Changeling Press LLC

ChangelingPress.com

Maui/Truth Duet
A Dixie Reapers Bad Boys Romance
Harley Wylde

Maui/Truth Duet
A Dixie Reapers Bad Boys Romance
Harley Wylde

All rights reserved.
Copyright ©2024 Harley Wylde

ISBN: 978-1-60521-889-2

Publisher:
Changeling Press LLC
315 N. Centre St.
Martinsburg, WV 25404
ChangelingPress.com

Printed in the U.S.A.

Editor: Crystal Esau
Cover Artist: Bryan Keller

The individual stories in this anthology have been previously released in E-Book format.

Table of Contents

Maui (Savage Raptors MC 3)
A Dixie Reapers Bad Boys Romance
Harley Wylde

Casey -- It's been a year since I showed up on my dad's doorstep with my *surprise, you have a daughter* bomb. He took me in. Gave me the first true home and family I've ever had. But now I want more. There's been one man who's always watching over me. Maui. He's one of the club's officers, and so much older than me. To me, age is just a number. Does he feel the same? Or is he only taking care of me because I'm his President's daughter? With Maui, I want everything, but will he want someone as broken as me?

Maui -- I told myself I was too old for her. Tried to just be her friend. Then I hear her screaming in her sleep, and I realize what types of monsters she's been fighting on her own. She needs me, and I need her. Whatever it takes, Casey and her baby will be mine. But first, I need to get a little bloody because there's no way I'm letting anyone live after they've hurt my family. I'll wipe them off the face of the earth so Casey won't be scared anymore. I hope she accepts the darker side of me. Either way, she's mine and I'm hers.

Prologue

Maui
Three Months Ago

I could still hear her screaming. In the middle of the night, I'd jolt awake, thinking I needed to save Casey. She didn't know I'd heard her. One of the times I'd helped with Becca, I'd sent Casey to bed, only for her to have a nightmare. We hadn't discussed it, but I thought I knew what she'd been through. I'd heard her pleas, listened to her tell multiple guys no. My gut twisted at the implication. Did Atilla know? I doubted it. If he had, those fuckers would have been buried already. Which meant she hadn't been dreaming like this at his house. What triggered them now?

I didn't need to overstep, and it could backfire in a huge way, but I also couldn't sit and do nothing. Calling Wire, I hoped like hell I was making the right decision.

"What's up, Maui?" he asked the second the call connected.

"Need a favor. You know Atilla's daughter, Casey?"

"Yeah, why?" The sudden tension in Wire's voice told me he felt protective of her. Good. She needed all of us standing behind her and ready to take down any monsters who threatened her or Becca.

"Think someone has hurt her. Maybe Becca's dad. When you were doing all that digging in the trafficking ring, did you notice anything out of the ordinary about the baby daddy?" I asked.

"I have his name but didn't really look into him. Casey said he'd not wanted anything to do with her or the baby, so I assumed he'd filled out the form willingly. Just a dumb teenage kid, you know?"

"I have a feeling it's more involved. Can you see if anything pops up on the little fucker?"

"Sure. Anyone else know about this?" he asked.

"No, and I want to keep it that way for now. She's been through hell already. We all have. I don't want to shake up the club if it's unnecessary. Atilla is settling into his life with Solena and the kids. Casey and Becca are living on their own, Meredith and Lynx have the twins to raise. No one needs this shit if it turns out to be nothing."

"Understood. I'll see what I can find. In the meantime, want to tell me what makes you think this kid did something wrong?"

I held back for a second. How much did I want to tell him? What if I was completely off base with this? Although my gut said I wasn't wrong.

"I believe he assaulted Casey. Possibly with more than one other guy. She had a bad nightmare not too long ago. I'm not sure if it was just a dream. Think she was reliving a traumatic experience."

"Fuck," Wire muttered. "All right. I'll focus on this and get Lavender to help. We'll call if we find anything, but you need to tell Atilla. I'm not going to have him come after me for this."

"Done. Just not until I know for sure there's anything to worry about."

We ended the call, and I shoved the phone into my pocket. Leaning against my bike, I folded my arms and watched Casey's house. Inside the compound, she should be completely safe. *Should* being the operative word. I'd have felt better if her house were at the back of the compound, far from the clubhouse. What if a party got out of hand? Or someone could slip through who wanted to hurt her or little Becca. I'd let nothing happen to either of them.

She was far too young for me. Only seventeen to my thirty-five. Hell, she could have been my daughter. But after seeing Atilla settle down with someone so much younger than he was, and Lynx pairing off with Meredith, it made me wonder if maybe Casey wasn't so far out of reach. Not now, clearly, but once she turned eighteen, maybe I could express an interest in dating her.

She was a new mom. I didn't want her to feel rushed, or like I was pushing her into a corner. If she wasn't ready, then I'd back off. Didn't mean I'd go away completely, though. I could be her friend, if that was what she needed most. For now, I'd keep watch. Protect her, even if she didn't think she needed it.

I heard Becca cry and nearly rushed inside to check on the little one. That darling girl had me wrapped around her finger, much like her mother. Rebel came around the bend and pulled to a stop on the road.

"You stalking her?" he asked, flashing me a smile.

The fucker knew exactly how I felt about her. The moment he started nosing around, I'd told him I wanted Casey to be mine. Someday. Thankfully, he didn't see her that way.

"Just making sure they stay safe," I said. "You heading home? Alone?"

He shrugged. "Same pussy as usual at the clubhouse. Getting tired of it."

I knew what he meant. I hadn't been with any of the club girls in over a year. Last time I'd gotten my dick wet had been months before Casey came to the compound. Once I set eyes on her, it was all over for me. I hadn't wanted anyone else since then.

The baby quieted, and I saw the shadow of Casey passing by the window. Atilla had given her this tiny home to share with Becca, and I'd heard he planned to give her the house he had now. His new home already had the foundation and frame up. Hopefully, it wouldn't be too long before the workers could complete it.

"You could let her know you're here," Rebel said. "Think she might welcome the company."

Maybe. But what if she didn't? I wouldn't want her to feel obligated to invite me inside. Rebel waved and pulled away, heading farther into the compound. I took a chance and pushed off from my bike, walking up to Casey's front door. I lightly knocked, not wanting to startle Becca since she was no longer crying.

Casey opened the door, her hair in disarray and dark smudges under her eyes. She always looked so exhausted, and my heart hurt for her.

"You want some help?" I asked. I saw Becca was still awake and sucking on her thumb. "Want me to walk with her?"

"Are you sure?"

"Yeah. You look ready to drop. Go get some rest. I'll get the little one back to sleep, then let myself out."

Casey smiled up at me. "Thank you, Maui. You're a lifesaver."

I stepped into the house and took Becca from her. Once the little girl snuggled against my chest, I rubbed her back as we walked back and forth from the kitchen through the small living room, and back again. If I didn't think the night air might be too much for her, I'd have taken her outside for a bit.

Casey yawned so wide her jaw cracked, and I watched as she stumbled her way back to the bedroom. I knew Atilla and Solena helped when they could, but it wasn't enough. She'd eventually get sick if she kept doing this on her own.

"Little one, you need to let your mom sleep more," I murmured to Becca. "You're exhausting her. What do you think will happen if she gets too sick to take care of you?"

The baby sighed and kept sucking her thumb. I looked down and realized she'd shut her eyes. Good. Maybe both of them would be asleep soon. The slight weight against me was a welcome one. I'd never thought of myself as a family man. Not until now. The more time I spent with Becca and Casey, the more I wanted to keep them forever.

I hoped like hell Wire didn't find anything on Casey's ex-boyfriend. Because if he did, I knew I wouldn't let that little shit keep breathing. Neither would Atilla. Only one problem. Casey hadn't told any of us about Becca's father, which made me wonder why she was protecting someone like that. One wrong move and the future I wanted could go up in smoke. I needed to tread carefully, but if he'd hurt her, I wouldn't let it slide.

Someone needed to make sure she and Becca could live a safe and happy life. If that meant getting blood on my hands, then so be it. There wasn't a damn thing I wouldn't do for the two of them. I'd walk through hell, give up my soul, or spend time in prison. None of it mattered. I'd give them my everything, if only Casey would accept it.

Becca slept soundly, so I crept to her crib and placed her gently inside. After checking on Casey, I let myself out, locking the door behind me. One day, I'd lock this door and stay inside with my girls. Assuming Atilla didn't rip off my balls for daring to covet his daughter.

One step at a time.

Protect Casey and Becca.

Confess my feelings.

Then hope like hell the Pres didn't murder me.

Chapter One

Maui

Everyone thought Casey would be excited to celebrate her birthday. The young woman I'd been watching didn't look like today was the least bit special. She'd been through hell. If anyone had a right to not feel like celebrating, it was her. She'd shown up at the clubhouse, seventeen and pregnant, and I knew it had been a big blow for her dad. The Pres had never mentioned having a woman, or a kid. I wondered how long it had festered inside him, hiding all the pain of losing his family.

During the time I'd spent with Casey since she arrived, I'd learned quite a bit about her. Like the fact she'd never really celebrated her birthday, wouldn't divulge the name of the guy who'd knocked her up, and she planned to live her life for her daughter. She'd taken on a lot of responsibility, and I'd done my best to help her shoulder some of it.

Which was why I found myself on her porch, with Rebel. Atilla and Solena had sent us over with a note. Basically, we were to let her pick who she wanted to spend the day with, then give her a memorable birthday. Just not memorable enough to have Atilla threaten our lives. He'd already made sure we knew what would happen if we touched his precious daughter.

"You going to knock?" Rebel asked.

"You do it." I was an asshole. Why did I make him knock? Because if we woke up Casey, I didn't want to be the one at fault.

She opened the door and looked like she might drop at any second.

"Hey, guys. Did Dad send you over to get me?"

Rebel flashed her his signature grin, guaranteed to drop panties, and I fought the urge to throat punch him. Instead, I shoved my hands in my pockets and let him dig his own grave. She didn't look ready to handle his bullshit today.

"You have a choice," Rebel said. "The note explains it."

He handed her the envelope. I knew what was inside. A birthday card from her dad and Solena, along with a message from each. I'd read it as they'd written it earlier. Atilla had kept things somewhat simple. *You have a choice to make. I asked Rebel to take you to dinner, dancing, and make sure you had the best birthday ever.*

Then there was Solena's message, which was why I hadn't dressed up too much before coming over. Unlike Rebel, who'd styled his hair, doused himself in cologne, and gone all out. Solena was on my side, and her message proved it. *Maui is there to give you whatever you really need for your birthday. I doubt it's a night out on the town like your dad thinks. But you should know both were threatened with death and dismemberment if they laid a hand on you.*

Casey snickered after reading the card. Good. She needed to laugh more.

"So, which of us will you be spending the night with?" Rebel asked, wagging his eyebrows at her suggestively. She shook her head at his antics. If he wasn't such a nice guy, I'd have been tempted to kick his ass right off the porch.

"I hate to disappoint you both, but..."

"You aren't up for going out," I said. That meant I had a better shot at spending time with her than Rebel. "When did you last sleep?"

"I sleep every night," she muttered.

"You know what I mean," I said. "Don't be a

smartass."

She sighed and rubbed her hand over her face. "Becca had a fever, and she's still having reflux. I still have to be careful if I don't want her to throw up her food."

"She's eight months now, isn't she?" I asked.

"Yeah. I'm starting to get her mashed up banana, yogurt, and other things like that. Those do better with her than the pureed baby food. Do the two of you want to come in?" Casey asked.

Rebel shook his head. Smart man. "I think I'll head out. I hope you've had a happy birthday, Casey. I'll take you out for lunch sometime soon."

Sure he would. Over my dead body. As much as I didn't want to be one of those asshole cavemen, when it came to Casey, all bets were off. I didn't like how close she'd gotten with Rebel. At the same time, I knew she needed the support of everyone around her. It felt like I was caught between a rock and a hard place.

He waved as he stepped off the porch and wandered off into the night. I studied Casey, wondering if she was still okay with me going inside. She'd never turned me away, but typically I came over to help with Becca. Tonight, it would only be the two of us. Lately, it felt like something was building between me and Casey, but I didn't know if it was wishful thinking on my part. Casey could have any man she wanted.

For a lot of people, the age gap between us would be too much. As far as I was concerned, it was just a number. Who the hell cared? As long as it didn't bother Casey, then I was fine with it. Her dad might take a little convincing, although he tried not to be too overbearing after not being part of her life for so long. As he often said, she'd grown up just fine without his input.

"You coming in?" she asked, taking a step back.

"Where's Becca?" I scanned the room as I entered her tiny home. Solena had mentioned babysitting. Had they already picked her up? I'd assumed it was only Casey at home right now, but it might not be the case. If Becca was here, I wasn't about to send her away.

"She's sleeping at Dad's tonight. Now I know why he took her." She patted my arm. "I really appreciate you wanting to take me out for my birthday. I'm sorry I'm not up for it."

"It's your day, Casey. Which means we do whatever you want. Looks to me like you need some help around here more than you need dinner and a movie. Although, there's no reason we can't still do that right here." I rolled up my shirt sleeves. She could relax while I cleaned, cooked, and prepared a special night for her.

"Are you sure you're okay with this?" she asked.

"Go take a hot bath or a nap. Your choice. I'll pick up around here and get dinner going. Any requests?" I asked.

"No. Anything is fine." She paused before going into her room. "Solena brought over a cake this morning. We can have some for dessert. It has fruit filling and whipped frosting."

"Already had some?" I smiled, picturing her digging into the cake. Her cheeks flushed, and she nodded. So damn cute. "Go relax. I'll call you when dinner is ready."

I picked up what little trash I found in the main living areas, emptied her kitchen garbage can, loaded the dishwasher, and dug through the cabinets to figure out what I'd cook. I'd just preheated the oven when my phone started vibrating in my pocket. I'd turned the ringer off, not wanting anyone to disturb my time with Casey.

Wire's name flashed across the screen, and I knew I needed to take the call.

"Find something?" I asked. It had been months, and so far, neither he nor Lavender had dug up anything. Except they said the guy's record was too clean, as in it had been doctored by someone.

"Maybe. We know who his closest friends were back then. They aren't quite as clean as Casey's ex. One is currently doing time for rape. Another left the country, and the third is still in the same town as Casey's ex. They have a beer together at least once a week."

"That's all?" I asked.

"Lavender has an idea who cleaned the kid's records. If she can get in touch with the hacker responsible, and feel him out, we might be able to put a few pieces of the puzzle together. Just don't hold your breath."

I whistled. "Man, you mean to tell me there's something the two of you *can't* do? I'm in shock right now."

"Shut it, fucker. We aren't getting any younger, and some of the fresh blood out there is nearly as good as we were at their age. Give them time, and a few might surpass us."

"Keep me posted. It's her eighteenth birthday today, so I'm at her place making dinner. If I don't answer, I'll call back when I can."

"Understood."

I ended the call and put my phone away before working on dinner again. I'd found bell pepper and onion in the fridge, as well as hamburger meat and shredded cheese. While Casey didn't seem to have any taco shells, I'd found some taco bowls. I baked them in the oven while I browned the meat and veggies, seasoning it enough to add some flavor without making it too strong for Casey. Cilantro lime rice was the next thing to start. Dinner might not be fancy, but I knew it was something she liked, since I'd made it for her before. Unless she'd lied to spare my feelings. Too late to worry about it now.

Once everything was done, I set the table and called out to her.

"Casey, dinner is done."

"I'll be there in a minute," she said.

I hadn't realized she'd come out of her room and gone into the bathroom until I heard the water sloshing before the sound of the tub draining. I cleared my throat and adjusted myself. The thought of her standing just one room away, and naked, had my cock's full attention. Last thing I needed was to sport wood when she came out of there. She might very well run screaming from the house.

Since I'd never cared much for sweet tea, Casey always kept some soda stocked. She'd offered to keep beer in the fridge for the times I dropped by, but I wasn't a big drinker. Not to mention I didn't want to drink around Becca. My brother had driven his car off the side of a winding highway, down an embankment, and into the ocean. He'd been drunk off his ass and the accident had kept me from alcohol for a long time. I had the occasional drink with my club brothers, but it didn't happen often.

I set out a soda for me and a glass of tea for Casey. She came to the table wearing an off-the-shoulder top and leggings. Barefoot. The woman was driving me crazy, and she wasn't even trying.

"Hope this is okay," I said, motioning to the

dinner I'd prepared.

"It's great." She smiled. "You know how much I enjoy your cooking. Although, I'd love it if you'd make something Hawaiian sometime. I want to try it."

"My mom sent me a few recipes recently. Maybe I'll pull them out and make a few dishes one day soon. We can have a picnic lunch with Becca."

Casey shifted in her seat. "Or we could eat here? Or at your place, although you might not want Becca there. She makes a mess."

"You really think I'm going to be upset if she spills something or throws up on the floor?" I asked. "Although I don't want her doing that last one. Not because I'm worried about my floors, but I don't like it when little Becca is sick."

"Same here." She took a bite of her food and hummed her appreciation. "This is so good. I can't tell you how much I love the fact I didn't have to cook tonight."

I stopped by at least twice a week. Should I have been coming to visit more often? Even when I was here, she seldom asked me to cook. Hell, most times I just did it because she looked too tired to handle it. She worked at the café and took care of Becca. I knew her dad kept an eye on her, and Solena helped when she could, but who took care of Casey and gave her some time to herself? No one. Well, unless you counted the times I could stop by.

I'd planned to take things slow with her, give her time to adjust to the thought of us dating. Maybe I needed to take a page out of Lynx's book and just tell her she was mine. Would she balk? Could she handle being with a man like me? I knew nothing about her ex-boyfriend. She hadn't even told us his name. Although Wire clearly knew it.

"You've been here a year now," I said. "Not once have you gone out on a date. Any reason why?"

"The right person never asked. Besides, I've been a bit busy."

"And if someone asked now?" I set my fork down and focused on Casey.

"Are you? Asking?" Her lips tilted up in a slight smile. "Were you waiting all this time for me to turn eighteen?"

I pushed my chair back and kneeled down beside her. Right now, she looked young and vulnerable. At the same time, there was a light in her eyes I hadn't seen before. Did the idea of me waiting for her make Casey happy?

"What if I said I wanted you and Becca to be mine? My woman. My daughter. Can you handle that?" She reached out and brushed her fingers over my cheek. I'd shaved a few days ago, but already had new whiskers growing in. I picked up her hand and kissed it, not wanting her to get whisker burn. "I didn't want to push you or make a move too soon. You're still young and have your entire life ahead of you. If you need to take things slow, then tell me."

A tear slipped down her cheek and she hastily wiped it away, then refused to meet my gaze. What the hell just happened? Had I fucked up? I stood and moved away, wondering if I should leave and give her space.

"Talk to me, Casey. Tell me what you need from me."

"I can't be yours, Maui." She sniffled. "I want to. More than you'll ever know, but it wouldn't be right."

What the fuck was she saying? If she wanted this, and I did, what else mattered? Did she think her dad would have a big problem with it? If he did, I'd talk to him. The man couldn't exactly say I was too old for her. There were fewer years between me and Casey than there was between Atilla and Solena.

"What's that supposed to mean?" I asked.

"I haven't been honest with everyone. I know how all of you feel about the women at the clubhouse. Would you still want me if I'm just as dirty as they are?"

I closed my eyes and clenched my jaw. There was no way she'd been anything like those women. If she felt like she wasn't good enough for me, then I had a feeling my fears were right. Her ex had done something horrible to her. That asshole needed to be buried.

"I want their names," I said.

"What?" She looked up at me again. "Names?"

"The boys who hurt you, who made you feel dirty. I want to know who did that to you, and then I'm going to make them pay."

"Why would you think…"

She couldn't even finish her sentence. She pressed her hand to her mouth to hold back her sobs. Going to her, I took her in my arms and held her. It didn't matter if Wire found anything. I didn't need his confirmation. Not anymore.

"Let it all out, baby. You don't have to hold it in." I kissed the top of her head. "You're so fucking strong, Casey. How the hell have you been holding onto that all this time?"

"If I were strong, it wouldn't have happened," she mumbled.

"Not true. There are different kinds of strength. If you couldn't fight them off, it doesn't make you weak. What it does, however, is make them dead. I meant it, Casey. I want their names. Every last fucking one of them."

"Does it really matter? It's in the past."

I held her another moment before taking a step back and making sure I had her attention. In the past? Like hell. She lived with this shit every day. It haunted her dreams. How could she even think of giving them a free pass? Besides, if they'd hurt her, how many others had suffered at their hands?

"Casey, I know you have nightmares about what happened. I've heard your screams. This is still very much a part of your present, whether or not you want to admit it. Did you stop to think they may have hurt other people?" I took a breath and came clean. "I knew something happened, even if I didn't have the details. My gut said some boys or men had hurt you. I asked Wire to look into things."

She paled and backed up, shaking her head. Why was she so scared? Who the hell were those pricks? It didn't matter. They could be the sons of the fucking president of the country, and I'd still go after them.

"He pulled the name of your ex off the forms he signed, the ones Su and Mark gave him regarding Becca being adopted. Then I asked him to look at the fucker a bit deeper, and his friends. Did you know one of them is doing time for rape?" She flinched and wouldn't hold my gaze. "You aren't the only victim, Casey."

I watched and waited. I knew Casey. There was no way she'd keep quiet if she thought other women were being hurt by those assholes. She'd speak up. Like I'd told her, she was stronger than she realized. It took courage to face this head-on, but she could do it. I'd hold her hand and walk with her every step of the way. Once I knew for certain which ones hurt her, I'd go after them... and I'd make sure they suffered.

Chapter Two

Casey

I hadn't planned to ever tell anyone what happened. During one of the many talks I'd had with my dad, I'd implied I'd only ever been with my boyfriend and just the one time. It wasn't true. Sure, my first time was with that monster. The second time, he'd drugged me. Not enough for me to black out. No, far worse. I'd laughed and had the grandest time, letting him take me in front of his friends, then not saying a word when they…

I swallowed hard, pushing back the memories. The drugs had worn off partway through, and I'd begged them to stop. None of them listened. How could I tell all that to Maui? He'd never look at me the same way. And what if he told my dad? I couldn't risk it. Although, it seemed he'd already asked Wire to dig up dirt on my ex and his friends. How long before the entire story came to light anyway?

"Can you ask Wire to stop looking?" I asked.

"Are you going to give me their names?" He folded his arms and waited patiently for my answer. Maui had never been one to push me. Until now. I had a feeling he wouldn't let this go.

"I don't want my dad to find out. He can't. Right now, he needs to focus on Solena and the kids. If he hears what happened to me, he's going to lose it."

Maui nodded. "You're right. He would. But if you give me their names, I'll keep this from him as long as I can. You know he'll eventually find out. Better to tell him."

"I can't." My voice cracked, and I knew I was about to cry again. "Please, Maui."

"Be mine, Casey. None of this changes how I feel

about you and Becca. Let me be the one to take care of the boys who hurt you. I'll handle everything before your dad even finds out."

I shook my head. "I can't let you do that. You know he'll be pissed. What if he kicks you out?"

"We can talk to him together after this is handled. No one else at the club needs to know, unless your dad tells them later. I can't control Atilla. No one can."

He wasn't telling me anything I didn't already know. The only person who had a prayer of holding my dad back was Solena, and I didn't want her to know either. She'd been through so much already. Besides, what if she felt betrayed by my silence over this? She'd suffered at the hands of her ex, but she hadn't hidden it from my dad.

"My ex-boyfriend's name is Seth Luton. The friends who were there that night are Chris Patterson, Dylan Tate, and Parker Griggs." I moved a little closer to Maui, reaching out for him. He took my hand and pulled me closer, wrapping his arms around me. Being held by him was the best feeling in the world. I closed my eyes, breathed in his scent, and found the courage to tell him what happened. It all poured out of me, and I had to admit when I'd finished, I felt better.

"I can't touch two of them. Not with my own hands at any rate. Chris Patterson is in prison for rape. Parker Griggs is out of the country. Makes me wonder if he's on the run before charges can be brought against him for something. I doubt it was the first or last time those assholes did something like that. As for the other two, Wire hadn't dug up anything yet. He said it looked like your ex paid a hacker to clean his records."

"He had money, so it's possible he'd do something like that." I looked up at him. "You really still want me, knowing all that?"

"Of course, I do. You still want me, knowing I'm going to tear those two apart with my bare hands and bury them somewhere?" He lightly touched my chin with his fingertips. "Because I'm not going to let them go easily. Their deaths will be painful and messy."

There was a time his words would have scared me. Now I knew about the monsters in the world, and I trusted Maui to protect me and little Becca. I also knew my dad's club wouldn't sit back and do nothing when it came to other men hurting women and children.

"Just don't get caught," I said. "I don't want you to claim me and then have to visit you in prison the rest of your life. None of them are worth a murder charge."

He grinned. "They may not be, but you are. And don't worry. I won't get caught."

His assurance, and cockiness, made me think he'd done something like this before. How many others had he protected? "Don't you need to ask my dad and the club for permission to claim me?"

"Technically, yes. Since I'm an officer of the club, it should be easier to get it pushed through. Your dad will be the deciding factor."

"I left my phone in my room. Can I use yours?" I held out my hand. He unlocked it, not bothering to hide his passcode from me, and gave the device to me. I called my dad, knowing there was only one way to guarantee his approval.

"Did she not pick you?" my dad asked the second the call connected.

"Um, Dad, it's me."

"Casey? Everything all right? Why are you using Maui's phone? Did something happen?"

I rolled my eyes. "Dad, calm down. I'm fine. I just didn't want to go grab my phone."

"You're home?"

"I was too tired to go out. Maui made me dinner here, and we're going to watch a movie. He took one look at me and knew what I needed most was time to relax."

He grunted. "Looks like he's doing something right, then."

"You know how you keep asking what I want for my birthday? I've decided."

"It's about time. So what is it you want? A new car? A vacation?" Dad asked.

"Well, both sound nice, but no. What I want is… Maui." The line was quiet, and I looked at the screen, wondering if the call had dropped. Nope. I'd just stunned my dad. "You're still there, right?"

"I'm here. I think I need you to explain that one a bit more. When you say you want Maui for your birthday…"

"He wants to claim me and Becca, Dad. And that's what I want too. I know I only turned eighteen today, but he's been here quite a bit since I moved into this house. Even before that, he helped me when he could. We've grown close since I came to the Savage Raptors."

I heard my dad scratch his chin through his beard. "So, he wants to claim you, but you're the one calling me? Did he lose his balls or something?"

I snorted. "No. Look, I know the club has rules. You claimed Solena without asking for a vote. I don't know how things worked with Meredith, or what will happen when the others find someone, but this is something I need. I need Maui, and so does Becca. I'm asking you to give your permission without the rest of the club being asked if they're okay with it. Because if they say no, it's going to feel like they've all stabbed me in the back."

"Jesus," he muttered. "Hit me where it hurts why don't you? Fine. You want Maui, he's yours. But I need to hear from him that he wants this too. It's not like I can just gift wrap him for you."

I handed the phone to Maui and went to cut a slice of cake for each of us while he talked to my dad. By the time he'd ended the call, he looked happier than I'd seen him. Ever. It seemed we had permission. I didn't have a clue what happened next, but this was a good start.

"You know, I heard Lynx's sister Ridley did something similar. She walked into Church at the Dixie Reapers clubhouse and claimed Venom in front of everyone. You're just as ballsy as she is."

"Not quite. I only called my dad."

"We'll have to agree to disagree. So… cake and then what? Movie?"

"Are you all right with that? Technically, we're a couple now." He'd said we could take things slowly. Did he still mean it? I hadn't been with anyone since that night, and while I knew things would be different with Maui, I wasn't sure if I was ready for that step right this second. I needed at least a day or two to adjust to being claimed by him. Or had I claimed him? I wasn't sure what my dad would tell the club. Would it bother Maui if everyone thought I'd laid claim to him?

He tipped my chin up and leaned in, giving me plenty of time to pull away. His lips brushed mine in a butterfly soft kiss before he retreated. It wasn't what I'd expected for my first kiss with Maui, and yet, it felt perfect.

"I told you we could do this at your pace. You're exhausted, Casey. Let's relax tonight, and in the morning, we can discuss the two of you moving into my house."

"Uh… You're aware my dad is giving me his house, right? I mean, the one he has now."

Maui nodded. "I know that. You've never been to my place. It's a little farther back, which means it's quieter. I think you'll like it. If you see it and can't stand the thought of living there, we can talk about moving into Atilla's place. However, with all the delays, there's no telling when he'll be moving into the new house."

I knew he was right. It seemed like one thing after another happened. Mostly rain. The electricians and plumbers kept getting called out on emergencies, and until the wiring and pipes were run, no one could hang drywall. Dad griped about it rather frequently.

"Will Becca have her own room?" I asked.

"Of course, she will. Do you think I'd try to move my family into a house smaller than this one? You've probably noticed each house in the compound looks like a log cabin. For the most part, they have a similar layout. However, those of us who were claiming a house right away had some input into our designs. It's why your dad's house doesn't look like the bulk of the ones here."

"And yours is different too?" I asked.

"Ours," he corrected, "and yes, it is. It has two bedrooms downstairs and two upstairs."

Now I wanted to see it. I hadn't realized we had two-story cabins. Were there others like Maui's? No, *ours*. It felt odd even thinking of his home as mine, but I'd get used to it. Eventually.

"What about a fenced yard? I didn't like the fact this one didn't have an area where Becca could play when she's older without me worrying about her darting into the road or wandering off."

"It does, and there's a reason for it. How do you feel about furry family members?"

"Um, like a cat or dog?" I asked.

"Not exactly."

What the hell kind of pet did he have? Waiting until tomorrow to see his place was sounding like a bad idea. I'd lie awake all night worrying about the sort of furry creature I'd end up living with.

"Want to watch the movie at my place?" he asked. "You can bring some things with you and stay the night, or you can come back here."

"You'd let me sleep here tonight even after claiming me?" I asked.

He shrugged. "We have our entire lives together, Casey. What's one more night apart? The last thing I want to do is scare you away by pushing for too much too fast. But starting tomorrow, we'll be living together. Now that you've talked to your dad and made everything official, you don't have a choice in the matter."

"That's fine. I wasn't planning for us to be apart tonight. Of course, I hadn't considered the fact you wouldn't want to sleep here."

"Can't leave Roscoe alone for too long."

I closed my eyes, wondering if I really wanted to know what the hell a Roscoe was. Better to find out now. Either way, I'd be living with it from now on. It wasn't like I was going to demand Maui get rid of his pet. Unless it hurt Becca, but I didn't think I'd have to ask then. No way he'd let anyone hurt his daughter.

My dad was the same way, which is why I didn't want him to know about Seth and the others. He'd go track them down, even the one in prison, and kill them. I couldn't do that to Solena.

"Let me eat my cake and then you can introduce me to Roscoe. I'm not going to get bitten, am I?"

He shook his head. "Nope. He's a sweetheart."

Only one way to find out.

I quickly ate my slice of cake, grabbed some essentials and tossed them into a bag, then followed Maui out to his bike. He took the bag from me and helped me onto the motorcycle. After swinging his leg over and sitting in front of me, he placed my bag in front of him.

"I'm going to go slow since you don't have a helmet," he said.

I clung to him, closing my eyes and enjoying the wind in my hair. Even though he couldn't have been going more than twenty miles per hour, it still felt like freedom to ride with him. I wondered if he'd take me on a real ride sometime soon.

Maui parked under the carport at his house and helped me off the bike. A set of double doors were in front of us, and I wondered what was behind them. I knew some homes had their laundry room outside in a space like that. Or was it storage? Plenty of time for questions. Right now, I needed to meet Roscoe, and figure out whether it was time to freak the hell out.

"Ready?" he asked, reaching for my hand. I gave him a nod and held on tight as he led me into the house.

I heard nails against the wood floors and braced myself. Nothing could have prepared me for Roscoe.

"Have you lost your fucking mind?" I asked, staring at his pet. "Seriously. Did you have an accident and have a TBI or something? Why the hell would you have *that* as a pet?"

Maui snorted, then released my hand to pick up the creature. "Careful, Casey. You'll hurt his feelings."

He scratched the chocolate skunk under the chin and cuddled it close. Yep. A motherfucking skunk. Who had something like that as a pet? I'd known he was somewhat crazy since he was part of this club, but I hadn't realized how bad it was until now. Was it too late to run for the hills?

"He's de-scented," Maui said. "So he won't spray you or the house. He has a play area, which keeps him from clawing up the doorframes, cabinets, and anything else that looks entertaining. Thanks to a talk with Doolittle, he even has a custom-made hideout. It's a cat cave covered in carpet, but larger than what you'd see in stores for cats."

"Sweet Jesus. A skunk. You seriously live with a skunk."

"No, baby. *We* do."

I whimpered and stared at Roscoe. He wasn't going to hurt Becca, was he? I had to admit he looked rather content in Maui's arms. Couldn't blame him. It was a rather awesome place to be.

Shit. I was now the mom of a skunk, and I didn't see any way out of it.

Why the hell didn't anyone warn me? My dad had to be laughing his ass off right now.

"Here," Maui held Roscoe out to me. "I promise he's not as awful as you think."

I reluctantly took the skunk and held it against me. I had to admit he didn't smell as bad as I'd feared. No worse than a dog who hadn't had a bath in a week. The little creature looked up at me. The trust in his eyes killed me. Whatever reservations I might have, it was clear Roscoe didn't have any.

"Hi, Roscoe. Looks like I'm your new mom."

He smacked his lips and snuggled closer. Maui winked at me, and I knew it pleased him to see his pet in my arms. Of all the things I'd contemplated having in my life, a skunk had never been one of them.

Chapter Three

Maui

I'd seen the horror in Casey's eyes when she got her first glimpse of Roscoe. Now the two were asleep on the couch. My pet skunk lay in her arms, looking utterly content. I wondered what he'd think of Becca, or how the baby would react to him. Roscoe hadn't had the chance to be around kids much. I knew Doolittle had worked with him a bit before I'd gotten him. He'd likely been around the children at the Devil's Fury compound, but I doubted any had been as young as Becca.

I knew I should wake her up and get her to bed. If she stayed on the couch all night, she'd end up with a sore neck. And yet, I couldn't bring myself to disturb her rest. Why hadn't she let more people help before now? I knew she had her pride, and could be stubborn as a damn mule, but at what expense? Did she really think wearing herself out was of any benefit to little Becca?

"If I'd stopped by more often, would you have let me help?" I mumbled. I doubted it. Most of the time, she'd tried to push me away, saying she was fine. It had only been my refusal to leave immediately that let me through her front door. Most didn't bother to push so hard.

I left the two of them alone, knowing Roscoe would move to his play area, eventually. He enjoyed sleeping in his pile of blankets. Knowing Casey, she'd want to give Becca the second bedroom downstairs. Right now, it remained empty. I'd had no use for it, even though I'd toyed with the idea of making it a play area for Roscoe. Instead, I'd turned the old laundry closet into his play area, after sealing off the hole for the dryer vent. One of the first changes I'd made to the house was to add on a laundry room off the kitchen. I hadn't had a pantry either, so I'd created a short hall with shelves for dry goods and cans, which led to the laundry area.

I hadn't had a chance to show it to Casey yet. I'd thought she might like having a designated spot for something like that. There was enough room for clothes hampers. I'd added a table for folding, and underneath were organizers for things like laundry detergent, dryer sheets, and anything else she might need. The table could also double as an ironing board in a pinch.

As I stared into the empty second bedroom, I wondered how quickly I could get things delivered for Becca. I knew she had a crib already, as well as a changing table. There had been little space at Casey's place for any extras. Now that Becca would have a normal-sized room, I wanted to make the area a haven for her.

I pulled out my phone and shot off a text to Ravager. The man did amazing work and enjoyed building things. No sense buying cheap stuff at the big box stores for my daughter when I could have something custom made for her.

I need two small bookshelves and a toy box for Becca.

Despite the late hour, he answered immediately, which told me he'd most likely been in his workshop and not at the clubhouse. The man liked to party, but not all the time. If anything, he seemed to find the club whores to be tedious.

Anything specific I need to include in the designs?

As small as Becca was, she hadn't really developed enough of her personality for me to determine what would suit her best. Instead, I decided to let Ravager be as creative as he wanted and told him as much. Whatever he came up with, I knew it would look amazing. I also trusted him to make sure there wouldn't be sharp corners since he knew it was for a small child.

Is there a color scheme in her room?

His question made me realize Becca's current room didn't really have much to make it unique. She had several themed blankets and sheets, and Casey hadn't decorated the walls yet. Or if she'd had something up, it hadn't lasted long. As protective as she felt over Becca, she may have worried pictures would fall and hurt her baby. I already knew I'd be bolting the bookshelves to the wall, and possibly the crib as well.

Shit. The toy box. What if she crawled inside it and got stuck?

Make sure she can't get trapped in the toy box. I probably didn't need to tell Ravager that, anyway. Since he knew it was for Becca, he'd ensure it would be safe for her. Everyone at the club adored the little girl. Even Meredith had started to interact with her. After she'd gone through a miscarriage, she'd had a tough time being around pregnant women or children. Then she and Lynx had adopted two kids, and things had improved for her.

I'll make sure it's vented and can't be locked.

Good enough for me. I couldn't wait to see what design he came up with. Knowing Ravager, the shelves and toy box would all match. It made me want to request a bed as well, but I didn't want to spend more on a crib when Becca could only use one for so long. At least the other items would carry her through her toddler years and beyond.

I hoped Casey wouldn't be upset I didn't give her

any input. Now that I'd claimed her and Becca, or rather my woman had claimed me, I wanted to jump into my role as Becca's dad and not hold back. I'd loved that little girl since the day she'd been born. I still had to deal with her sperm donor, as well as the other shits who'd hurt Casey. Atilla would be pissed as fuck when he found out, especially if I didn't let him know before I made my move. I'd take whatever punishment he gave me. I couldn't drag him into this when he'd just claimed Solena and had two adopted kids. Soon, there would be two more joining the family since Solena discovered she was carrying twins.

Would Casey want more? We hadn't discussed it. As much as I wanted a baby with her, I'd be content if Becca was our only child. I'd been there for Becca from the beginning. It wasn't like I'd missed out on the first eight months of her life. We'd have to tell Becca she wasn't my biological child, once she was old enough, for medical purposes if nothing else. I didn't want our life to be built on a lie. Although, in every way that counted, she was mine.

"What are you doing?" Casey asked, coming up behind me. I hadn't even heard her.

"Thinking about our daughter."

She wrapped her arms around me and smiled. "I like hearing you call her that. Becca loves you already. You know that, right?"

"I do. I should have asked you first, but I asked Ravager to make some furniture for Becca. This will be her room, and it's going to look empty with the few things she has now. The man is a genius when it comes to woodwork. He's going to make a set of bookshelves as well as a toy box."

"Don't spoil her too much," Casey said. "We don't want her to be rotten."

"Don't worry. I won't let her turn out like Venom's girls. Or did you not hear about that?" I asked.

"No one's said a word. Why would they? Isn't he with the Dixie Reapers? I know Lynx is related to one of them somehow, but what does that have to do with the club?"

"Let's go curl up in bed and I'll tell you the story of Meredith and Lynx's relationship. Or the parts I know. I'm sure you heard about her miscarriage, and that's why she didn't want to see Becca."

"Yeah, I knew about that, and I understood."

Of course, she did. Casey was a sweetheart, and she'd never hold something like that against someone. I'd known women who would have been pissed about Meredith refusing to see their kid. Not my woman. I spent the next half hour telling her how the two met, what Meredith went through with her mental illness, then losing the baby, and how she'd been treated by the club she'd called family.

"So Venom's girls live with the Devil's Fury?" she asked.

"Yeah. Farrah is with Demon, and Mariah is with Savage. I always thought they were sweet girls, until this. I can't believe how they acted. Venom and Ridley called them on their shit and made them leave the compound. They took Lynx and Meredith's side because their kids were acting like little bitches." I smiled. "Can't say I'd have handled it any different. So you don't have to worry about me spoiling Becca too much. I don't want to have anything like that happen in the future with her."

"Good. I have a hard enough time getting my dad to give her things in moderation. I know grandparents are supposed to spoil their grandkids, but I think he'd take it too far if I let him."

"There's something else we need to discuss. You know I need to leave before too long. I can't let your ex and his friend off the hook. I also plan to see what connections I have inside the prison where Chris is being held. The one out of country will be more difficult, but not impossible."

She sighed and closed her eyes. She might understand why I needed to do this, but I also knew she was worried about me. Whatever it took, I'd make sure she didn't keep having nightmares about what happened. If that meant burying those bastards, then so be it. Honestly, I was looking forward to it. I wanted them to hurt, to hear their screams and pleas for mercy, and laugh in their fucking faces. They hadn't cared if they hurt Casey or degraded her. Why the hell should I be merciful to them?

"When?" she asked.

"I'm going to get you and Becca moved in here first. Need the club to know the two of you are mine, so not for at least a few days. Maybe a little longer. I may ask Wire to track Seth's and Dylan's daily movements. The more I know about them, the easier this will be."

"And the sooner you can come home," she said.

"Right."

"As much as I don't want anyone else to know what happened, I don't like the thought of you handling this on your own. What if something goes wrong?"

I kissed her forehead. "I know, baby."

Since our club wasn't the only one who didn't like rapists, I wondered if I could get some help outside of my brothers. I wasn't sure how to go about it. Not without Casey's situation coming to light. Although, I did have two options to consider. Casper VanHorne and Specter. I'd need to contact them to get help with the fucker who'd fled the country. Maybe they knew someone in the area who could lend a hand with the two I'd be taking out on my own.

I wasn't going to discuss any of it with Casey. For one, I didn't want to involve her in this if I didn't have to. The less she knew, the better. Second, if I talked to her about my plans, then she might expect it when it came to other matters. And club business would never be up for discussion.

"When I come back, you can let me know if you're ready for us to take the next step. There's more we need to discuss before then anyway."

"Like what?" she asked.

"My past history with women, and the fact I'm clean. Whether we want more kids, and when we might want them. If you still want to work at the café or stay home with Becca. What you think life will be like as my woman. That's just to start."

"All right. We can start those conversations tomorrow. I think I'm too tired to tackle anything big like that. Although, the first one sounds settled already. It's not like I thought you were a virgin. I'm not going to demand a list of names or something. Not even sure I want to know if you've been with the women who currently hang out at the clubhouse."

I'd been with two of them. It had been a long while ago, and I had a feeling those women wouldn't linger much longer. They were getting older, and my brothers had tired of them. Made us all sound like assholes. Maybe we were. Sometimes the women at the clubhouse stuck around for years. Other times, it was a fleeting thing, and they were gone after one or two parties. I thought they liked claiming to have slept with one of us, or just wanted to taste life on the wild side.

"You have your GED now, don't you?" I asked. I remembered her studying for it, but I couldn't recall her actually going to take the test.

"Yeah. Why?"

"If you don't want to keep working at the café, but think you might want a job later, would you consider applying for college?"

She leaned up on her elbow to look down at me. "What? Me? College?"

"Why not? You're smart, Casey. If you don't want to go to a campus to take classes, there are plenty of places that offer them online. I'm not saying it's something you have to do. I only tossed the idea out there in case you were interested."

"I'll think about it," she said. "Right now, being Becca's mom is more important to me. If you're serious about me quitting the café, then I'll take you up on the offer. I won't feel so run down all the time if I can rest more during the times she's napping."

"Then it's settled. Call the café in the morning and give your notice. If you need to cover more shifts while they hire someone else, I'll help you watch Becca."

"And what if you have to go do something for the club?" she asked.

"Then we check with someone else here. You know Becca has an entire club who would gladly watch over her, right? Hell, Rebel might be a cocky asshole on the best of days, but I'm sure he'd even watch her if we asked him to."

"With so many kids here now, maybe what we really need is a club babysitter." She smiled and snuggled against me again. "Except, I doubt too many parents will let their teen daughters come here, especially at night."

"Probably not."

The club needed to make a lot of changes. It was time for us to adapt. Some of us had wanted to settle down and start families, which was a large part of why Atilla built this compound. But it hadn't looked like any of us would find our one and only anytime soon. Which meant we didn't have things set up to make this a family friendly place to live.

I had no doubt the Pres had a few ideas already. Wouldn't hurt to ask him about it. I couldn't recall discussing it in any detail during Church in the last several months. Since he had elementary-age kids, and Lynx had the twins, it would be a good idea to have a place where they could all play together. What if someone else found a woman who already had children? We needed a neutral area for the club's kids to play together. Otherwise, we'd likely have chaos and children running everywhere.

Although, that didn't sound terrible. I'd visited some of the other clubs like the Dixie Reapers and even the Hades Abyss. I liked the way they had things set up and enjoyed the overall feel of their compounds. I knew Atilla felt the same.

A light snore nearly made me laugh. I looked at Casey and realized she'd already fallen asleep again. Her lips were slightly parted, and she looked fucking adorable. Knowing I'd get many more nights like this filled me with joy. If someone had told me five years ago I'd have a woman and daughter, I'd have told them to shut the fuck up. Now I had Casey and Becca, and I'd do whatever it took to keep them safe. Even kill the bastards who'd hurt Casey.

Chapter Four

Casey

Moving into Maui's house really did make the most sense. I'd thought it would be easier for him to adapt to what Becca and I might need, but I hadn't counted on Roscoe. Knowing he had a pet changed things. The skunk seemed sweet. However, at the end of the day, it was still an animal, and I wasn't sure what behavioral issues we might face if we uprooted Roscoe from his home.

Becca was small enough she wouldn't notice the changes. As for me, I couldn't remember the last time things had been stable in my life. Even once I'd moved in with my dad, there'd been the chaos with Solena and the kids. Although, we'd had a lot of quiet moments, I'd also had Mark and Su hanging over my head. Rolling with the punches was just one of my many talents. All right, maybe not *many*.

I sat on the floor with Becca between my legs and little Roscoe staring at her from two feet away. He hadn't known what to think of the baby, and while Becca seemed curious about the furry creature, she hadn't tried to make a grab for him. Her behavior surprised me. I'd expected her to want to hold the skunk. Of course, I didn't have any pets and neither did my dad. She hadn't had the chance to be around animals.

"What are my girls doing?" Maui asked, lounging against the doorframe.

"I'm waiting for Roscoe to make a move. So far, he's keeping his distance."

He winked and came closer, scooping up Roscoe. Holding the skunk close to his chest, he kneeled in front of us and reached for Becca's hand. He held it in his, letting the skunk sniff her before placing her chubby fingers on his dark fur.

"Are you sure he won't bite her?" I asked.

"He's relaxed," Maui said. "I'll keep her safe."

"I know you will." I leaned toward him. Maui met me halfway, and I pressed my lips to his in a brief kiss. "There's still a lot we haven't discussed, but I don't think I can handle it all at once."

"We have all the time in the world."

"Have you asked my dad for time off yet?"

He sighed and sat on the floor, letting Roscoe go. Reaching for Becca, he pulled her into his arms and stared at me over her head. "Not yet. I spoke with Wire this morning. He said to give him a few days and he'd have more information for me so I'm not going in blind."

"You could just let it go," I said. "Or ask him to turn everything over to the police."

"Still don't trust me to stay out of jail?" He smiled. "Can't leave my two girls, not when I just managed to claim you. Some other guy might swoop in and steal you away."

I crossed my arms. "Last time I checked, I told my dad I wanted you for my birthday present. Think that means I claimed *you*."

"That you did." He kissed Becca on the cheek, then set her down. She immediately went to her hands and knees. She'd managed to crawl a little, but she wasn't mobile enough I needed to worry just yet. Maui reached over to take my hand. "Only one little issue."

"What?"

"You keep calling me Maui. When the others are present, that's fine. But when we're by ourselves?"

I nodded. I knew Solena had permission to call my dad by his real name, even though it was super rare for her to actually do it. From what I'd heard, that was her choice and not because he'd forced her to call him Atilla. I figured it was the same for Meredith and Lynx.

"So what's your real name?" I asked.

"Koa Akana. Both my parents and grandparents were Hawaiian. According to my mother, one of her grandparents emigrated from China."

I remembered him saying his family were no longer living. Although, he hadn't gone into detail. Since he wasn't very old, I had to assume something happened like an accident or illness.

"Koa." It suited him. There were days I could picture him on a surfboard easier than I could on a motorcycle. Although, I had to admit I enjoyed seeing him in his leather cut, jeans, and biker boots. The man made my heart flutter no matter what he had on. "Do you miss Hawaii?"

"Sometimes. I'd like to go visit. Take you and Becca with me."

"I've never been to the ocean before," I said. "It looks beautiful on TV and in pictures."

"There's no comparison to seeing it in person. What do you say we take the little one to the park? She likes the swings, right?"

I nodded. "The park off Main Street has a baby swing. The one closer to us doesn't."

"Then let's head over there, and when she's tired, we'll take a break and get something at Spill the Beans."

"I need to change." His gaze skimmed over me from my messy bun to my off-the-shoulder shirt and my leggings, down to my bare toes. The heated look in his eyes said he thought I looked fine just as I was, which made my cheeks warm.

"Just put some shoes on. We'll have to take your

car." He stood and picked up Becca again. "I'll get the princess ready and get her bag."

Seeing my small daughter held against his broad chest did funny things to me. My heart skipped a beat, and my breath caught. Why did he look so sexy with a baby in his arms? I watched them leave the room, then fell backward on the floor, staring up at the ceiling. I was in so much trouble. How would I ever survive being around him every single day?

Roscoe scampered over and booped me with his nose. I scratched under his chin before heaving myself up off the floor. While Maui got Becca ready, I went to get my shoes from the bedroom. After I slipped on my Converse, I used the bathroom, put on a tinted lip balm, and spritzed on a little perfume. I couldn't very well walk around looking like a complete train wreck while a man stood beside me who looked like a sex god. Well, I could, but I knew women would come hit on him.

Was I ready for that? Probably not. But Maui had chosen me, and that meant something. I couldn't let other women get to me. If he'd wanted someone else, he wouldn't have moved me and Becca into his house. No, *our* house.

"Ready?" he called out from the hall.

"I'm coming. Let me grab my keys."

"I have them. You left them in the kitchen."

Of course, I did. I didn't even remember having them in there. No one told me when I had a baby I'd lose half my brain cells. I couldn't remember much of anything these days. I followed Maui and Becca out to the car, and while he buckled her into the baby seat in back, I got into the passenger seat and fastened my seat belt.

I tried not to laugh when Maui banged his knees

on the steering wheel, let out a few curses, then slid the seat back. His head brushed the ceiling of the car. He really wasn't built for something this small. My dad kept trying to give me an SUV, and I'd been stalling. I knew he wanted to make up for lost time, but it felt like he was trying to buy my affection -- which wasn't true. Not even a little.

"I'm buying a truck," he said. "Unless you tell me you want three or four kids. Then I'll get a big-ass SUV to haul everyone around."

"Can you really just decide you're going to go buy a vehicle?" I asked. We hadn't discussed finances. He'd said I could stay home with Becca, but I hadn't thought to ask the details.

"I'm not a millionaire or anything, if that's what you're asking. As an officer of the club, I make a larger cut than most. We can live comfortably even if I buy a truck and you quit your job. Speaking of... have you done that yet?"

"I called them this morning. I offered to stay until they hired someone, but the manager said there was a stack of applications in the office. Sounds like they have it covered. Which means I'm officially a stay-at-home mom now."

He leaned over to kiss my cheek. "Good, then we can work on getting rid of the dark circles under your eyes. I don't like the fact you were running yourself into the ground instead of asking for help. Try that again and I'll spank your ass."

I'd try to do better, but... I still wasn't used to having a support system. Mark and Su had only acted like they cared. The more I thought about my time with them, I had to wonder if they'd wanted to sell me too. Why had they kept me all that time? Too much visibility? Everyone in the area had known my grandparents. It wouldn't do me any good to sit here and wonder about it now.

Maui found a place to park not too far from the swings, and we got out of the car. I grabbed Becca's bag, and Maui unbuckled our daughter from her baby seat. He carried her to the swings, and the moment she saw them, she started to kick her feet. I hadn't had the space for a baby swing at home, and now that she was getting so big, I didn't see the point in getting one. Although, I had seen one we could hang in the yard. It would be easier than bringing her to the park all the time.

Maui placed her in the swing, fastened the safety straps, then gave her a gentle push. Becca babbled at him and swung her fist around. I hid my smile behind my hand, knowing my baby girl was telling him to go higher. She was a fearless little thing. When she started to fuss, Maui gave a soft growl and pushed her a little harder. Becca squealed and kicked her feet.

"Is she always like this?" he asked.

"Pretty much. This is her favorite thing to do. She even likes it more than her toys at home."

"Looks like we need to get a swing, then. I know she's still too small for a play set, but it wouldn't hurt to get one. We could always take off one of the regular swings and hang a baby one there until she's older. It won't be long before she can use the slide, with a little help."

"Maybe we should double-check the fencing first. Make sure she won't be able to escape when she's more mobile."

We spent the next thirty minutes at the park with Becca, and when she started to yawn, Maui stopped the swing and held her in the crook of one arm, while reaching for my hand. I laced my fingers with his and let him lead me over to Spill the Beans.

"Know what you want?" he asked.

"Raspberry white mocha with extra whipped cream. A hot one."

He placed our order, getting a black coffee for himself, then found a table for us. By the time they called his name, little Becca slept soundly against his shoulder. I stood and hurried to the counter to grab our drinks and noticed more than one woman checking him out. I couldn't blame them. Maui by himself was sexy as hell, but holding our daughter? Yeah, it made him downright lethal to a woman's heart.

I set his coffee down in front of him and retook my seat. I'd enjoyed our outing. While he'd helped with Becca before, this was our first time doing something as a family. I only wished I'd had a way to commemorate the moment with a picture. As if hearing my inner thoughts, Rebel and Truth entered the coffee shop. I waved them over and held my phone out to Rebel.

"Can you get a picture of the three of us?" His eyebrows rose, but he didn't say anything. It seemed my dad hadn't informed the club about my new status yet. I didn't know how everyone would react. Scooting my chair closer to Maui's, my big, sexy biker put his arm around me and we smiled as Rebel snapped our picture. "Thanks!"

I looked at the image on my phone and set it as my background. Our first family picture! I couldn't wait to take more.

"Send that to me," Maui said.

I texted it to his phone, and noticed Rebel and Truth were still standing by our table. I glanced up and saw the smirk on Rebel's lips, and the furrow of

Truth's brow. It looked like Rebel had figured something out, or thought he had. As for Truth, he clearly didn't know why Maui and I were here with Becca.

"The three of you having fun?" Rebel asked.

"Yeah. We took Becca to the park." I took a sip of my drink and licked the whipped cream off my lip. "She loves the swing."

"I didn't realize the two of you hung out so much," Truth said, his gaze flitting between me and Maui.

Maui's hold tightened on me. "Why wouldn't I be out with my family?"

"What?" Truth scowled. "What the hell is that supposed to mean? There's no fucking way you're…"

Rebel punched him in the arm and hissed out a *shut the fuck up.* I knew what he'd been trying to say. Since I'd been knocked up when I came to the Savage Raptors, it wasn't possible for Maui to be Becca's birth father. Except he didn't seem to care. Maui had claimed her as his daughter, and I didn't think he'd like Truth trying to tell the world Becca wasn't his. I looked up at my biker and saw the thunderous expression on his face. Yep. Truth was going to be in for it.

"The two of you came here for a reason," Maui said. "I doubt it was to ruin my day. Get on with your business. And, Truth? Stay the fuck out of mine."

Rebel shoved at Truth, pushing him away from us and toward the counter. He waved at us over his shoulder, and the tension slowly drained from Maui.

"You know he won't be the first to say that," I said.

"Well, I guess if I start knocking out their teeth, the rest of them will catch on fast."

He made a good point, although I hoped it didn't come to that. Then again, if my dad heard what Truth said just now, he'd probably beat the shit out of him.

"Let's not tell my dad about this," I said.

"Oh, no. That I can't do, baby. He needs to know about Truth's attitude. It's not the first time he's done something like this. Some woman really fucked with his head, and ever since, he tends to lash out at any female he thinks is stepping out of place. The club whores are fine, unless they start asking for more."

"Maybe he'll learn one day," I said.

"If not, we're going to have a big problem. I'd thought he was doing better, but then he says or does something stupid and proves me wrong."

"We shouldn't let him ruin our day out. Let's finish our coffee. We can stop by the grocery store and get the ingredients I need to bake cookies, and I can cook pork chops with rice for dinner."

He gave me a nod and drained his coffee cup. I sipped on my mocha a little longer, wanting to savor it. Truth and Rebel were gone by the time we left. We drove over to the grocery store, grabbed enough ingredients for multiple meals, and went home. It was the first time I'd shopped with a guy who wasn't my dad, and I had to admit I liked it. Doing everyday couple things felt nice.

Chapter Five

Maui

I'd hated leaving Casey and Becca behind. We'd spent an incredible few days together, bonding as a family. But I'd made myself a promise. It was time to take out the trash who'd dared to lay a hand on my woman. I'd already scouted the area and knew exactly when I'd get rid of Seth and Dylan. Since I was alone, I wouldn't be taking them on at the same time, which meant I had to plan everything carefully.

I pressed my phone to my ear and waited for Casper VanHorne to answer. Although, his greeting did make me smile.

"Who the fuck is this and what the fuck do you want?" he asked when the call connected.

"My name is Maui, and I'm with the Savage Raptors. I'm hoping you can help me out with something or tell me who can."

Casper grunted. "Fine. Tell me what it is, then I'll decide."

I explained what happened to Casey, and how one of the assholes had fled the country while another was rotting in prison. Neither of which I could reach on my own. They needed to pay. Eventually, Chris would get out. When he did, it would only be a matter of time before he'd hurt another woman.

"I admit I'm intrigued," Casper said. "I'm also retired. Promised my wife I wouldn't take on any more jobs."

"Then do you have an idea who could handle the problem overseas?"

"I'll have Specter call you. I'm not sure where he is right now. If he's not in the US, he may decide to handle that little fucker himself. None of us like rapists. And if he's unable to take care of the problem, he can find someone who will."

"What's it going to cost me?" I asked.

"A favor. At some point in the future, whoever accepts the job may ask for your help. Are you willing to accept those terms?"

"I am." I'd have agreed to pretty much anything. "Let Specter know I'm dealing with two of the men on my own. If he calls and I don't answer, it means I'm otherwise occupied."

I heard Casper's soft laughter as the call dropped. I had a feeling he knew exactly what I meant, and how I felt. How many men had died at his hands? Mine might be covered in blood, but I knew he'd rid the world of far more people than I ever had. Although, the men and women I'd killed had raped, murdered, tortured, and done other unspeakable things to innocent people. They were worse than the monsters in horror movies. They didn't kill out of a need, or because it was some beastly instinct. No, they did it for pleasure.

I went over the encrypted files from Wire, and decided I'd handle Dylan first. As eager as I was to get my hands on Seth, I knew I'd be taking my time with him. Once I had Dylan out of the way, then I could haul Seth off to the kill room I'd set up. Thank goodness for old, abandoned structures. It hadn't taken long to track down a piece of land long forgotten by the family who owned it. Set back in the wooded area, I'd discovered a one-room cabin, deteriorated and falling down. Behind it had been a barn, still standing even if many of the wooden slats were long gone.

Not one single human footprint or tire print had been left behind, which meant no one had been there for a long while. No homes or businesses were within miles of the property, which meant the screams of Dylan and Seth wouldn't be heard.

The only thing I needed now was for the sun to set. In the cover of darkness, I'd track my prey, haul them off to the empty barn, and make sure they never hurt another woman again. If the police got hold of me, they'd arrest me for murder. As far as I was concerned, I was doing the community a favor. They hadn't bothered taking out their own trash, so I'd do it for them.

Dylan still worked the same job he'd had in high school, remained friends with Seth, and hadn't seemed to change much. I'd make sure to help him with that later tonight. In fact, no one would be able to recognize him once I'd finished.

My phone rang. Even though I didn't recognize the number, I answered.

"This is Maui," I said, when the call connected.

"Casper VanHorne asked me to call you."

Specter. It had to be. "Need some help."

"Boy, you need more than *some*. I figured you'd asked some of the hackers for help. Called Wire first, so I didn't have to move further down the list. Do you understand exactly what pile of shit you've stepped in?" Specter asked.

"Apparently not. Care to explain it to me?"

"Seth Luton. His uncle is Governor Mitchell Luton. When that boy disappears, people are going to search for him. His family isn't going to just let it go." Specter sighed. "I get why you want to kill him. Wire and Lavender said his family hired one of the best hackers in the world to cover up all his indiscretions. They've kept their precious boy out of trouble all these years."

Sounded like I needed something more than just his death. It wouldn't be enough. The last thing I wanted was for trouble to come knocking on my door. If they somehow did trace this back to me, I didn't want Casey to suffer for it.

"I need to talk to my woman. I have an idea, but I can't follow through without knowing she's fine with it."

"Look, Maui. I'm in the States. Give me three hours and I can be there. Don't go after Luton before then. Can you do that much for me?" Specter asked.

"Sure. But Dylan is fair game, right?"

"Yeah. Go have fun with that little pissant. Save the bigger fish for later. Don't forget you have something to lose now, Maui."

If I didn't, I wouldn't be here. As much as I wanted to say I was doing this for some altruistic reason, I'd be lying. I simply wanted vengeance for what they'd done to Casey. Sure, the end result would be getting these rotten men off the streets, which would keep them from harming other women. But that's exactly what it was... the *result* of my revenge.

"Casper might not want to get his hands dirty anymore, but I don't have anything holding me back. My baby sister will be taken care of. She's the property of Charming so she has the Devil's Boneyard to defend her. It's not like I have a woman or kid."

"I have the feeling if your sister heard you imply you have nothing to lose, she'd be furious."

He laughed. "Yeah, you're right about that. She's surprised me quite a few times over the years. Mostly when she picked Charming and asked him to hide her away. Fucker didn't realize she was my little sister."

"Now that's a story I need to hear sometime. If you're coming here to help, you should visit my club before you head out. They aren't too far down the highway."

"Does Atilla know what you're up to?" he asked.

"No, and there's a reason I didn't tell him. My woman, Casey, is his daughter. He'd lose his shit if he found out what she'd been through. Until now, she's never told anyone what happened to her. She only confided in me after I said I wanted to claim her. Silly woman tried to tell me she wasn't good enough, all because of what these fuckers put her through."

"We'll make them pay, Maui. We just need to handle things with Seth a little more carefully than with Dylan."

We ended the call, and I went over everything I knew about Dylan again, and knew it was time. He'd be getting off work soon. I needed to sabotage his car, then wait for it to break down. As much as I loved my bike, it wouldn't work for the job ahead of me. Instead, I'd bought a clunker off someone for five hundred dollars. I only needed it to run well enough to finish this job, then I'd ditch it.

It didn't take me long to reach Dylan's place of employment. I already knew what he drove, and where he liked to park. Since he stayed out of the view of the cameras in the lot, it made things easier for me. I broke into his vehicle, popped the hood, and tampered with his drive belt. It would still hold, at least long enough for him to hit the stretch of road going to his house outside of town.

Once he had no choice but to pull off onto the shoulder of the highway, I'd grab him. I had a syringe in my pocket, ready to go. Just enough to knock him out for me to move him to the old barn. Once he came to, the fun would begin.

Getting back in the clunker, I drove just outside of town and pulled off onto a dirt road in the darkness. And waited.

It didn't take long before Dylan drove past me. I eased onto the road, keeping my headlights off, and followed at a distance. I saw the moment he lost control of his car and knew the belt must have snapped. Pulling off onto the shoulder, I got out and walked to where Dylan now stood beside his car, cussing a blue streak.

The fucker didn't even notice my presence. I walked up behind him, stuck the needle in his neck and depressed the plunger. His knees buckled, and he was out. I capped the needle and shoved it back into my pocket to dispose of later, then hefted Dylan over my shoulder. I dumped him into my back seat and drove closer to the barn I'd prepped.

Inside, plastic covered the floor and walls. A wood chair sat in the center of the room, with a roll of duct tape and a small table for my tools. Once I had him strapped to the chair by binding his wrists to the armrests and his ankles to the legs with the duct tape, I sat back and waited for him to wake up. Looking at my phone, I realized Specter should be arriving within the next hour and a half. Plenty of time for me to destroy this little shit.

It took a while, but Dylan finally roused from his stupor. He blinked and looked around, his head bobbling a bit. I didn't want to hurt him too much, not until the drugs wore off a bit more. I wanted this asshole to feel the pain I inflicted.

"You finally awake?" I asked.

"Who're you?" he asked, his words slurring a little.

"Not important."

"What's going on?" He tugged at the tape holding his hands down to the chair. "Look, if you want money, I don't have any."

"Nope. It's not money I want." I leaned in a little closer. "I want your blood. Your pain. Your fear. I'm going to make you plead for mercy, just like she did."

He froze in place, his eyes going wide. At least the pieces were starting to click together in his head. Although, I doubted he knew I meant Casey.

"I don't know what you're talking about," he said after a long pause.

"Oh, I think you do." The longer I looked at him, the sicker I felt. Did Casey not realize the truth I'd just discovered? Or could she not bring herself to admit it? Because little Becca didn't belong to Seth Luton. I'd be willing to bet everything I had on this motherfucker being the one who knocked her up. "Casey. Name ring any bells?"

He paled and audibly swallowed. "What about her? She dated my friend back in high school. Got knocked up and moved."

"I know all about the baby, and what happened to Casey. I know about you, Seth, Chris, and Parker raping her. Did you really think you'd never pay for what you did?"

"Why do you care?"

I pointed to my cut. "See this?"

He nodded. "Yeah, you're a biker. What does that have to do with anything?"

"The president of my club is Casey's father. Be thankful I didn't tell him about your misdeeds. Although, I was somewhat selfish and wanted to be the man who ends your miserable life. You're not leaving this barn tonight, Dylan. At least, not in one piece." I smiled when he pissed himself. Good. I wanted him scared. Terrified. Ready to do anything to survive. And I did mean *anything*. I wanted to give him hope that he'd make it out of here, only to crush it beneath my boots and snuff out his life. "And in case I forgot to mention it, Casey is *mine.*"

"Shit," he whispered before whimpering like a small child.

"Let's get started, shall we?" I approached the table, where I'd laid out some tools. Picking up the pliers, I decided we'd start with his hands. "Oh, and before I forget, you can scream as much as you want. No one will hear you."

"Please! It's not what you think. Seth is the one who started it all! He insisted she wanted it. Even fucked her in front of us."

"She'd been drugged. Not enough to make her pass out, but just a large enough dose it made her too weak to put up a fight."

I gripped his index finger and grabbed hold of his nail with the pliers, then pulled until it came off. He screamed and cried, snot ran down his face. At this rate, he wouldn't make it through everything I had planned. After I removed all ten fingernails, I cut his clothes off his body. The idiot had no idea what was in store for him.

My phone buzzed in my pocket, and I paused long enough to check it. Specter's number. I opened the message and saw it led to an encrypted video. The man worked fast, or he'd already been planning to act before I'd even spoken to him. Of course, he could also have some excellent hackers working for him, like Wire and Lavender, or even better. If such persons existed. I recognized a prison when I saw one, which meant it had to be Chris pleading for his life. I turned up the volume so Dylan could hear. The whiny ass little shit just cried harder as he listened to the prisoners brutalize his friend.

One of the inmates came closer to the phone

recording the incident and smiled. "Don't worry. We'll take extra good care of him. About the time he heals, we'll teach him a lesson again. He's going to get a taste of his own medicine, until it fucking kills him."

"Make him suffer," I murmured, even though they couldn't hear me. I'd make sure Specter paid those men accordingly, or I'd do it myself. Their commissary accounts would be overflowing.

I shoved the phone back in my pocket and stared at Dylan. The hope had died in his eyes. Now that just wouldn't do. I'd wanted him to beg more. He'd been too easy to break.

"You're weaker than her," I said. "Even after what the four of you did to her, she's still standing strong. Then again, she's a biker's daughter and my old lady. Wouldn't expect anything else. You, however, are a little cockroach. The only thing to do with roaches is step on them."

I spent the next hour slicing Dylan with my knives, cut off a few of his fingers, and finally shoved my blade through his dick and balls. I watched him bleed out from his wounds, and wished I could have made him suffer even more.

"Damn, son. Remind me to never piss you off."

I spun to face the intruder, and realized he must be Specter. I also saw Seth, unconscious at his feet. Looked like it was time to clean up this mess and start on my next victim. But first, I wanted to know what Specter had planned. He'd said we had to do this carefully. I didn't give a shit who Seth Luton's uncle was. The man wasn't leaving this place alive. I'd do time if I had to. Anything to make sure Casey's rapists would never harm another soul ever again. *Sorry, baby. I may have to break my promise to return home to you.*

Chapter Six

Casey

Dad crossed his arms and stared me down. A lesser woman might have flinched. Not me. I'd gotten used to this sort of thing. Being surrounded by a bunch of bikers wasn't for the weak willed or faint of heart.

"Daddy, that isn't going to work."

He sighed. "I just find it odd Maui asks for time off, and then he leaves you and Becca behind. I'd thought he wanted to take the two of you on a family vacation or something. Of course, I'd have preferred to hold Church first and let everyone know you'd claimed him as your birthday present."

I pressed my hand to my mouth so I wouldn't laugh. He really would do it too. Poor Maui. "You know very well he claimed me first. I only asked to have him for my birthday so you wouldn't say no."

"Well, I may or may not let the others know about it. I rather like the thought of my daughter being enough of a bad ass to lay her claim on one of my bikers." He smiled faintly. "You're all grown up. Got yourself a man, a baby... not sure you need your old dad anymore."

I huffed and rolled my eyes. "Daddy, stop being ridiculous. I will *always* need you. Even when I'm your age, I'll still need you in my life."

"Honey, when you're my age, I'll be dead. It's just a fact." He came closer and pulled me in for a tight hug. "But even when I'm no longer part of this world, I'll still be watching over you."

My throat grew tight. "Like Grizzly and Meredith?"

He nodded. I hadn't been here for everything that happened between Meredith and her adopted family, but I'd heard about it. She'd lost her father and hadn't been able to repair her relationship with her sisters or the Devil's Fury. There were times she'd get a look in her eyes that made me wonder if she missed them. I couldn't imagine having sisters, then losing them.

"Nothing to worry about right now, honey. I've got a lot of years left in me."

He'd better. It had taken me seventeen years to find him. We had so many missed years to make up for. Plus, he had Solena now, and little Nora and Santiago. Plus two more babies on the way. Becca would need her grandfather. And… what if Maui and I had more children?

"Can we talk about something happier?" I asked. "Because you're going to make me cry."

"Sorry, honey. Now, let's get back to this situation with Maui. You really not going to tell me where he went?"

If I told him, then I'd have to explain what he was doing there. And by doing that, I'd have to tell him what happened to me. I didn't want to see the look on his face, for him to feel responsible. And I knew he would. He'd blame himself for not being there, for not asking why I didn't have a grave beside my mother's. We'd talked about that stuff before, and I knew he was eaten up with guilt. None of it had been his fault. My grandparents had been to blame.

"It's not like him to be so secretive. He's not in trouble, is he?" Dad asked.

"No, Daddy. He just said he had some business to take care of. Something personal. I think he plans to return tomorrow or the day after. He said it wasn't far away." Half-truths were the best I could do right now. But if he kept asking questions, I might slip up and say something I shouldn't.

"Well, whenever he comes back, I'll hold Church and let everyone officially know you belong to Maui now. Although, I'm pretty sure the entire club already knows you've moved into Maui's house."

"Oh, so now I belong to him and not the other way around. Careful, Daddy. Better make up your mind. Can't have your club thinking you're getting old."

"Shut it, you little brat." He patted me on the back and went to sit at the kitchen table. "Now... I don't suppose there's a beer in this house?"

"Nope. Maui doesn't want to drink alcohol in front of Becca."

"Can't even say I'm upset about that. I'll take some sweet tea, then."

I poured us both a glass and handed one to my dad. Taking a seat across from him, I wondered how long he planned to stay. Normally, I loved getting to visit with him. Just not when I was trying to keep a secret. I'd never hidden something from him before. Well, okay. So I'd not said a word about what happened to me. But this was different. Maui had pushed me until I'd spilled everything, and now it was all fresh in my mind.

"I can tell when something is bothering you," he said. "I've got no idea what Maui is up to, but it's clear you don't want me to know about it. I'm just not sure if it's because *he* didn't want you to say something, or if he's off doing something for you and you're too embarrassed to tell me about it."

"I'm not trying to lie to you," I said.

"Just tell me one thing. Is he doing something dangerous? Do I need to worry about it coming back on the club?"

I didn't know how to answer that. To me, yes, what he was doing was dangerous. I worried it would land him in prison. Maui, however, didn't seem concerned.

"He said everything would be fine." There. I'd told the truth. Part of it anyway.

"Casey, we may have only been part of each other's lives for a year now, but I think I know you pretty well. Talk to me, honey."

"What if it's something I can't tell you?" I asked. "What if telling you could potentially put you and your new family in harm's way? Even though Maui said it would all be fine, there's a small part of me that worries something will go wrong."

He took a swallow of his drink and studied me. I wished he'd look away. If he kept that up, I might very well crack and confess everything. Then I'd have to see the utter despair on his face, and deal with his fury. Because I had no doubt he'd rip Maui apart if he knew why he'd left town.

"Fine. Keep your secrets for now. When Maui comes back, I'll get the truth out of him. And, honey, I'm not going easy on him."

I didn't like the sound of that. What would happen to Maui? My dad wouldn't throw him out of the club, would he? Or worse? Was there something he could do that would be more severe than that? I didn't know, and I hoped I never found out.

"You and Becca need anything while he's gone?" Dad asked.

"We're fine, Daddy. The house is stocked with food. There's gas in my car. Maui will return soon."

"And if he doesn't?" he asked.

I'd been trying not to ask myself that. What would Becca and I do if Maui never came back? Even though I'd only been his for a short time, I didn't want to think about having to live without him. I wouldn't go so far as to say I loved him. It was too soon for that, but I did feel something for him. He'd been so sweet to me, and so good with Becca.

"He went to take care of something. Someone." I twisted my hands in my lap. "Becca's biological father. Maui wanted to make sure that man would never try to come for Becca. Even though he was going to sign away his rights for an adoption through Mark and Su, Maui worried he might change his mind later."

Dad leaned back in his chair, the wood creaking under his weight. "And you told him who Becca's sperm donor was?"

"Yeah, I did. Now that we're officially a couple, it seemed like the right thing to do. I'm not sure what he plans to accomplish…"

"I do," my dad muttered. "Fuck. He's going to kill the bastard."

"What? How did… I mean, *why* would you think that?" Did he catch my slipup?

"Because it's what I would have done if you'd ever given me his name."

Great. Not only was my boyfriend off killing the men who'd hurt me, but my dad was all gung ho to do the job himself. Now I understood why Maui had kept him in the dark. I mean, it was one thing to consider my dad would want to avenge me, and another to flat out hear him admit it. And he didn't even know what the asshole had done, other than knock me up. It would be worse if he knew the entire truth.

"I'm concerned he'll do something that lands him in jail," I admitted. "But he didn't want me to tell anyone, and insisted he could handle it on his own."

"He can, and he will, honey. Have some faith in him. Doesn't mean I won't chew his ass out when he comes back. You're my daughter and he should have talked to me about this."

"I didn't want him to."

"Mm-hm." He tapped his fingers on the table. "You're still hiding something from me. Keep your secrets for now, but I *will* find out what's going on. When I do, we're going to have a discussion about what you should and shouldn't do."

"I know there are rules to follow, and you've been lenient with me since I came here. Just don't be too hard on Maui, Daddy. He's doing what he thinks is right, and he didn't want to upset me. When I asked him not to tell you, he said he couldn't keep it from you forever."

"At least he's not a complete moron," he muttered. "Fine. I'm going to head home to Solena and the kids. Since you're here all alone, why don't you come to dinner? You know she always makes plenty on the off chance you stop by."

"I can do that. I'm sure Becca would love to see everyone. If you'd come to the house a little earlier, you'd have gotten to hold her. She'd just gone down for her nap a few minutes before you showed up."

"It's fine. I should have called."

"You know you're welcome anytime." My cheeks warmed. "Well, maybe not quite *any* time."

He stood so fast he nearly knocked the chair over. "On that note, it's time for me to leave. There are some things a dad doesn't need to know about his daughter. Far as I'm concerned, my granddaughter hatched out of an egg."

He wasn't technically wrong. She *had* come from one of my eggs.

"All right, Daddy. We'll see you later for dinner. Make sure you let Solena know we're coming. I don't want to take her by surprise. Isn't she due any day now?"

"They can't seem to narrow it down. They've changed her due date multiple times."

"I hope she has a safe delivery. As much as I want to be there for the two of you when she goes into labor, I'll stay with Santiago and Nora. It would be better for them to remain at home until after the babies are here. Maui and I can bring them to the hospital whenever Solena is ready for them."

"Sounds good, honey. I know she'll appreciate that." He kissed my forehead. "Get some rest and try not to stress too much."

"Love you, Daddy."

"Love you too."

I walked him out and locked the door behind him. He knew more than I'd wanted to tell him, but at least I hadn't told him everything. I wished Maui would hurry back home. I didn't know how many more rounds I could go with my dad without spilling everything.

Dinner would be interesting. I hoped like hell Solena ran the conversation, or the kids. Anything to keep Dad off the subject of Maui.

Please hurry home. I need you, Maui.

Chapter Seven

Maui

"Specter, I presume," I said. The man gave me a nod. "And that must be Seth."

"It is. He made it almost too easy to grab him. Fucker is cocky as shit. Thought he could best me because he's so much younger. Clearly, experience won."

While the kid was unconscious, I didn't see any visible bruises. If Specter had beaten him, he must have only hit him in places I couldn't see. Or he could have drugged him, but I doubted it. The way he'd phrased it made it sound like he'd taught the kid a lesson for underestimating him. Of course, I still wasn't sure what he had planned for this little shit.

"Where did you pick him up? Do we need to worry about retribution? You said his uncle was a politician." He'd told me to be careful and not make a move without him. So why had he snatched Seth without me? Had he worried I'd fuck it up?

"Wire called and told me where to find him. The second my plane touched down, there was a car waiting. I went to the bar where he'd found Seth through the security feed. The dipshit was posturing and acting like a big shot. I riled him up a little, and next thing I knew, he wanted to take things outside."

I shook my head. The kid really was dumb as shit. Anyone could look at Specter and see the man was a killer. It was in his eyes, and the way he carried himself. Everything about him screamed *don't fuck with me*.

"As to the other…" He nudged him with the toe of his boot. "I have a plan."

"Which is what?"

"We're going to video his confession. We don't even have to bring your woman into this. He's hurt many women. Took Wire and Lavender some time, but they were able to uncover the shit he'd had buried. More than a dozen rapes, and those are just the ones who accepted a payoff. Who knows how many more remained silent?"

"Thought they said they couldn't access any of it?" I asked.

"Well, they tracked down the hacker responsible. Apparently, Lavender tore into him for covering up something like this, then Wire threatened him. And not in the hacker way, but more in the *my club is going to murder you* sort of way."

"I think I can speak for the Savage Raptors when I say we'd like in on that. I can't stand pieces of shit like these. None of my brothers can."

"Only monsters could turn a blind eye to that sort of thing."

I waved a hand at Dylan's body. "Haven't cleaned that up yet. Think this one will freak out when he sees his buddy has been tortured and killed?"

"Doubt it. I don't think this one has emotions, other than anger. While he's out, let's do something about Dylan and strap Seth to the chair." Specter pulled his shirt over his head and tossed it into a clean corner of the barn. Even though he had to be a decade or more older than me, the man clearly still exercised on a regular basis. Yeah, Seth had been a dumbass to think he could go up against this man. "I'll call in a cleanup crew when we're done but might as well make things a little easier for them. Got anything that will work for dismemberment?"

"Not with me. Have a few knives that are good for smaller appendages like fingers and toes, but if you're thinking about removing arms and legs, we're going to need a bone saw or something." I wondered what the average person would think of our conversation. I smiled a little, picturing the look of stark terror on their faces. Yeah, I was a bit fucked up, but at least I only took out the trash. It wasn't like I went around killing innocent people. And this time it was personal.

"That look right there... Don't ever let your woman see it. She may know you're off killing her rapists, but seeing the joy you've taken in what you did to Dylan and what we're about to do to Seth, that's something else. She probably can't handle it. Not many can." He paused. "Except Jordan over at the Devil's Boneyard. That woman is something else. I think even I might be a little scared of her."

"World renown assassin Specter is scared of a woman?" I couldn't hide the humor in my voice. I hadn't personally met Jordan, but I'd heard stories about her. He wasn't the only one who wanted to avoid her. A lot of bikers spoke about her with both reverence and a bit of fear.

"I'll let the crew know they'll have to tackle that part too. I wasn't prepared for this sort of job when I left home and didn't have time to go back before heading your direction."

I took that to mean he'd come here from another job. I wasn't about to ask. Not my business, and I had a feeling the less I knew about it, the better.

We managed to get Dylan tucked away off to the side, then strapped Seth to the chair. I saw the lump on the back of his head and understood how Specter had subdued him. Unfortunately, he'd hit him hard enough he hadn't woken up yet.

"Think he'll be out much longer?" I asked.

"Not sure. I didn't think I hit him quite that hard.

Maybe he's more of a pussy than I'd even realized." Specter tapped Seth's cheeks, trying to rouse him. Eventually, the fucker opened his eyes.

"What the hell?" Seth's gaze narrowed on us. "The two of you better let me go. If you don't, my family is going to sue the shit out of you and toss your asses into jail."

"Son, the only one in this room truly deserving of prison time is *you*." Specter pulled out his phone, accessed an app, and then approached Seth. "Now, here's what's going to happen. You're going to confess to the multiple rapes you're responsible for. I'm going to send the video to the media outlets, along with the records your family tried to bury."

His nostrils flared and his eyes darkened with fury. Looked like he hadn't counted on someone getting the upper hand. Then again, people like him usually didn't. They thought their money would always protect them.

"You can't do that."

Really? That was the best he had? "Oh, we can, and we will. You're going to pay for your crimes, but don't be fooled. It won't be from the cushy insides of a prison cell."

"What's that supposed to mean?" he asked. "And why the hell do the two of you care about some bitches I've fucked?"

It took everything in me to hold back. I wanted to punch the motherfucker, but Specter had kept his face free of bruises for a reason.

"Remember your ex-girlfriend, Casey?" I asked. "She's the reason I'm here. For me, it's personal. But the man you should be most scared of is here because he doesn't like garbage like you. One less rapist in the world sounds pretty good."

"Is that what she told you? That I had to rape her?" Seth threw his head back and laughed. "What a lying little bitch. She opened her legs up just fine. No force needed."

Specter placed a hand on my chest, clearly knowing I was seconds from detonating. I took a step back, then another. I gave Specter some space, and after a few well-placed blows to Seth's abdomen, and one to his knee, the little shit was ready to talk.

"Fine! I'll make your damn video. But when my family gets their hands on you, you'll be sorry."

I pointed to Dylan's body. "You'll be joining him pretty soon. So if you think you can go running to your parents, you're wrong."

He looked in the direction I indicated. When he swung his gaze back to me, I realized Specter had been right about this one. There was nothing in his eyes. Entirely blank. We'd be doing society a favor by taking the fucker out.

I stood back as Seth spilled his guts about multiple rapes. The eager expression on his face as he relived the moments sickened me, even more so than hearing the details. The little bastard really did get off on it. Even now, he sported wood.

When he'd finished, Specter tapped on his phone screen, then showed me he'd sent the encrypted video to Wire. I knew the hacker would get it into the right hands, along with the documentation he'd found to back up Seth's crimes, and his family's coverups. It looked like Governor Luton would be going down soon. No way he'd be able to remain in office after this.

"Why do you give a shit about that bitch, Casey?" Seth asked, watching as Specter picked up one of my knives.

"Because she's mine. And her daddy is the

President of my club. Be thankful he's not here too. I don't think you'd have had enough teeth to speak clearly in order to record that video. Not that you'll be keeping them much longer."

Specter cut Seth's clothes off and removed his shoes, then sliced the soles of his feet. I didn't have to ask why. If the asshole managed to escape somehow, he wouldn't be able to run very fast or very far. Although, he would leave a blood trail we'd have to clean up.

"Have at it," Specter said, waving a hand at Seth.

I picked up the bloody pliers I'd used on Dylan and gripped Seth's jaw. Forcing his mouth open, I pulled his teeth, one at a time, until the bastard didn't have any left. Blood poured from his mouth and down his chin. He glared at me, but the fucker wouldn't give me the satisfaction of crying out in pain.

"Well, this isn't as much fun as I'd hoped," I said.

"I know you want him to suffer, but I don't think he'll give you much." Specter came up beside me, arms folded. "He's a different sort. One of the true monsters you don't run across very often. I'd suggest you vent your anger, and we move on. He's not going to beg you for mercy."

Shit. I knew he was right, but I didn't like it. I'd wanted this asshole to cry and contemplate the pain he'd caused Casey. Didn't look like I'd get my wish. Instead, I grabbed one of my larger knives and hacked and slashed at him. His blood pooled on the ground under the chair, and the spatter sprayed several feet in every direction. I knew I was wearing a good bit of it. I'd need to clean my cut and possibly burn my clothes. Couldn't go home to Casey like this.

Not once did Seth utter a single sound. I cut out his tongue, removed his fingers, and finally watched him bleed out as I sliced open his ball sac. Even the carnage I'd caused hadn't settled the beast inside me. I still wanted to hurt him, to make him pay for what he'd done to my woman. His death hadn't been enough.

Specter placed a hand on my shoulder. "No way we could disguise this as anything other than a crime of passion. I'll make sure the cleanup crew knows to burn the body, then scatter his bones in graves across the state."

"When you say graves…"

"Two of the men on the crew also dig graves for a few cemeteries. They'll put the bones under any new burials. No one will find him, even if they dig up those caskets because he'll be about another foot down."

"That's rather devious," I murmured. I liked it.

"Go get cleaned up and head home to your woman and daughter. I'm sure your President is curious what you've been up to. The question is whether you should tell him or get your woman to have a heart-to-heart with her daddy. Might come across better from her. He's going to be pissed you took away his chance to get revenge on the men who hurt his daughter. But if she talks to him and tells him why." Specter shrugged. "Might douse his fury."

He made a good point. I just wasn't sure if Casey would be up for it. I wouldn't press her to do something she wasn't ready for. She'd lived with this for more than a year, keeping it all to herself. Who was I to demand she tell her dad about the trauma she'd suffered? As her man, she was my first priority. Her emotional and mental well-being were part of that, not just keeping her physically safe.

"I'll ask her what she'd like to do," I said.

"Get out of here. I'll handle everything from this

point forward. And Casper said to let you know he's put a tail on Parker. It won't be long before he joins the others in hell. You can rest easy knowing you accomplished what you set out to do, even if it didn't turn out exactly as you'd hoped."

"Thanks, Specter. You ever need anything, let me know."

I shook his hand, then left the barn. The clunker needed to be taken care of before I went back to the motel. I parked it outside an apartment building on the seedier side of town, leaving the keys in the ignition. I double checked for blood, but in this area, I doubted anyone would report it. Someone would come along and claim it for their own. It might be a piece of shit, but it was better than no transportation at all.

The walk to the motel wasn't far, and thankfully it was dark enough no one noticed the blood on my clothes. When I got to my room, I stripped and got into the shower. As much as I knew I should get rid of my clothes, I didn't have a safe way to do that here. Instead, I bagged them up, and shoved them into my saddlebags. Then I hit the road and headed for home.

It was nearly three in the morning when I pulled through the gates of the compound. I gave the Prospect a quick wave before going straight to my house. The lights were off, which wasn't surprising. I hadn't let Casey know I was on my way back, and she was no doubt asleep. Entering the house as quietly as I could, I took my bloody clothes and shoved them into the washer, then started the machine.

I took the time to clean my cut and my boots before walking through the house in nothing but my underwear. Even though I'd showered at the motel, I wanted another one. Not only to get the road dust off me, but to make sure I didn't have a single drop of blood on me from Dylan or Seth. I wouldn't contaminate Casey by touching her before I'd scrubbed a second and third time.

I was on my second rinse when I realized I wasn't alone. She stood outside the shower, staring at me through the glass. I pushed the door open and reached for her, lacing my fingers with hers. "I'm fine, baby. Go back to bed and I'll be there soon."

"Is it over?" she asked.

"For the most part. You don't need to know the details. Dylan and Seth are dead. The other two will be joining them before too long. They'll never touch you again."

A tear slipped down her cheek and she hastily wiped it away. Releasing my hand, she pulled her nightshirt over her head, then shoved her panties down her thighs. My cock went hard in an instant, and I felt like such an asshole for noticing her sweet curves at a time like this.

She stepped into the shower, and I pulled her into my arms, holding her and giving her what comfort I could. I'd slayed two of her demons, but it would take time for her to realize she was truly safe now.

"Everything's going to be all right, Casey."

"I know," she murmured, then looked up at me. "Now I need you to do one more thing for me."

"What's that?"

"Give me some good memories so I don't equate sex with what happened to me. Wipe away their presence in every way possible, Koa. That's what I need from you."

I leaned down and kissed her, devouring her lips like they were the sweetest candy. If that's what she wanted, then I'd give it to her. For Casey, I'd do anything.

Chapter Eight

Casey

It's only Maui. It's his arms holding me. His body pressed against mine. There's no one here who will hurt me.

Even though I wanted him, and needed to be with him right now, part of me kept reliving the night with Seth and his friends. I knew I needed to get past it, and for me, that meant taking this step. If I didn't do this now, I might lose my courage. Realistically, I knew not all men were like Seth and the others. Maui would never do anything to cause me pain. Not intentionally.

"Are you sure?" he asked, backing me against the shower wall.

"Yes. I need this, Koa. I can't heal without it."

He went down to his knees, then lifted my legs over his shoulders, opening me up. I tensed for a moment as he spread my pussy lips apart, and I felt his hot breath against me. The first swipe of his tongue was a shock. The second had my muscles relaxing. It wasn't long before pleasure started to build, and I found myself gripping his hair and pressing his face tighter against me.

He sucked my clit into his mouth and worked a finger inside me, pumping it in and out. When his teeth scraped the swollen bud, I cried out, bucking against him. He doubled his efforts, and I came so hard, I nearly saw stars.

I'd thought he'd stop, but he didn't. He added a second finger, stretching me. Even though I'd given birth eight months ago, I felt the burn.

"You're so fucking tight," he murmured, licking me again. "I can't wait to feel you wrapped around my cock. You have no idea how badly I want you."

"Then take me," I said.

"Bed. We need to move to the bed. Our first time together shouldn't be in the shower." He pulled my legs off his shoulders and stood, bracing his hand on my hip to keep me upright. "You're not some club whore, or easy pussy from a bar. You're my woman, and I want to treat you right."

"Next time. Don't make me wait. Not right now."

He groaned and lifted me. I put my legs around his waist, and I felt the head of his cock brush against my pussy. He pushed inside me, and I held my breath as I stretched to accommodate him. I didn't know much about dicks, but his felt thicker than what I assumed to be the average.

"You okay?" he asked.

I felt his cock flex inside me and I nodded. Gripping his shoulders, I hoped he wouldn't change his mind and stop. I held his gaze as he slowly thrust into me, each stroke making those same sensations build again. I knew it wouldn't be long before I was coming.

"You need me to stop, say so."

"Keep going," I said.

He reached between us and rubbed my clit. Every swipe of his thumb sent shockwaves of pleasure through me. When I finally came, I saw the heat flare in his eyes and knew the second his control snapped. He held onto me, pinning me tight against the wall, as he fucked me hard and fast. He drove into me like a man possessed, not stopping or slowing.

He groaned and I felt the heat of his release. I'd thought that would be it. But not with my Maui. No, he kept going, his hips slapping against me. He shifted, changing the angle, and every stroke pushed me closer to something I'd never felt before. The feelings building were so intense they nearly frightened me.

I screamed as I came, and felt the gush of my cum. I not only soaked myself, but him as well. My cheeks warmed when I realized I'd squirted. I'd always thought that only happened in books or in porn. No one had ever told me it was a real thing.

"Oh my God, I…"

"That was fucking hot," he said right before kissing me breathless. "Are you sore?"

"I don't think so." My heart hammered in my chest, and I squeezed his cock with my inner muscles. He pulled out, and I felt his cum slide down my thighs.

Maui took his time cleaning us both, then led me to the bedroom. Instead of getting dressed in a fresh set of pajamas, he tossed me onto the bed, flipped me onto my stomach, and lifted me onto my knees.

"Spread them wide. I'm not done with you yet."

I fisted the covers as I obeyed his commands. He held me open and licked my pussy, his tongue flicking against my clit. He sucked, nipped, and teased me to orgasm three more times before his heavy body came down over mine. He flattened me to the bed, my thighs still spread wide.

Maui thrust against me, his cock brushing my clit with every stroke. I whimpered and squirmed under him, wanting so much more. Now that I'd had a taste of him, I didn't think I'd get enough. My cheeks warmed again as I realized he'd turned me into a woman mindless with her need for sex. Or rather, sex with him. I didn't think it would have been this intense with anyone else.

"If you want my dick inside you, come for me again, baby. Give me that cream, and I'll fuck you so good you'll still be feeling it tonight."

Tonight? I turned my head to look at the bedside table clock. Four in the morning? We wouldn't have long before Becca would wake up needing her diaper changed.

He bumped my clit again and I came, just as he'd wanted. The feel of his cock shoving inside me made my toes curl. He gripped my hair, forcing me to hold his gaze. As he took me with a ferocity I hadn't expected, I realized what he was doing. He was erasing the memories, just as I'd asked of him. My eyes burned with tears at how sweet Maui was, and I fell for him even harder.

He kissed me as he came inside me. Afterward, he cleaned us both up with a wet washcloth then held me in his arms. "That wasn't too much?" he asked, smoothing my hair back from my face.

"No. It was just what I needed."

He pressed a kiss to my forehead, and I closed my eyes, letting sleep pull me under. Not once had I been scared, like I'd thought would happen. I hadn't had any flashbacks while he'd been inside me, or holding me down. For the first time since that night, I felt like I might actually be free.

"Thank you," I whispered.

"Anytime, baby."

* * *

I rushed around my dad's kitchen, trying to help Maui as he prepared a Hawaiian dinner for everyone. Every now and then, I paused and tried not to wince. I might have told him I wasn't sore early this morning, but hours later? Totally different. I almost felt raw, and my jeans were definitely chafing.

Maui leaned in close to whisper in my ear. "Better stop getting that look on your face. It makes me want to strip you naked and bend you over."

"Would you stop?" I playfully smacked his arm. "My dad is in the other room!"

"Pretty sure he doesn't think you're a virgin, or that we haven't slept together."

"I can hear you," my dad yelled from the other room. "And I don't *want* to hear it, so shut the hell up."

Maui snickered and I wanted the ground to open up and swallow me. I'd never been so embarrassed in my life. He finished cooking while I set the table. I'd asked what he was making, and he said it wasn't a traditional Hawaiian meal but was the closest he could get on short notice. Teriyaki chicken topped with pineapple slices and served with a side of Hawaiian fried rice and Hawaiian rolls. Solena had already made dessert, and from the scent when we'd walked in the kitchen, I thought she'd made a coconut cake.

"Dinner," I called out. The kids rushed in first, with my dad following. He guided Solena into the room, his hand on her lower back. She really did look ready to pop at any moment.

"It smells great," Solena said.

Everyone dug in, and the conversation flowed well. Until my dad decided to lob a bomb at Maui.

"I found it odd you asked for time off, then disappeared while my daughter and grandchild were left here. If you didn't need time for a family vacation, where the hell were you?" he asked.

What the hell was my dad up to? The way he phrased it, and the look in his eyes, said he knew Maui had been up to something illegal. And while I hadn't told him what my biker had been doing, I'd given enough away he'd known it could be something bad. But why was he starting this in front of the kids? Was he really that pissed about it?

"I never said I was taking them somewhere. I told you I had something personal to take care of."

My dad glared at him, and I had a feeling this

wouldn't end well. Before we came here, Maui had asked if I wanted to tell my dad what happened to me, or if I wanted him to do it. At the time, I'd said he should. Why? Because I was a coward. He might call me strong, but I wasn't. I couldn't bear the thought of hurting my dad and knew my confession would tear him apart.

"I lied before," I said softly. "I knew where he was and what he was doing, but it's not something we should talk about right now."

Dad paused with his fork halfway to his mouth. I couldn't hold his gaze, but the tension in the room increased by a million. He might not know what I was going to say, but he could tell it wasn't something good. Plus, I'd admitted to lying to him. I knew he wouldn't like it. In fact, he was probably both hurt and pissed right now.

We finished eating, and Solena herded the kids from the room.

"We'll have cake after I get the kids ready for bed," she said. "They can go ahead and take their baths and put on pajamas."

I looked to where Becca sat in her highchair. She was too young to understand what was going on, but I didn't like the thought of talking about this in front of her. Maui stood and kissed the top of my head. "I'll take her to the other room. Talk to your dad and if you need me, give a shout."

"Or you can put her in the playpen and bring your ass back in here," Dad said.

"Or I could do that," Maui agreed. He picked up Becca and left the room with her. I shifted in my chair, still unable to look at my dad. When Maui returned, he sat beside me and took my hand.

"Start talking," Dad said.

"There's something I've kept from you. A lie by omission."

"For how long?" he asked.

"Since I came here," I whispered. "I was too ashamed to tell you. I only confessed to Maui because I'd refused to let him claim me. When he pressed me for an answer, and I told him why we couldn't be together, it opened up old wounds and I..."

A tear slid down my cheek. Maui lifted me onto his lap and put his arms around me. I snuggled into him and tried to gather the courage to tell my dad the rest. My story spilled out in bits and pieces. When I'd finished, I had tears streaking my cheeks.

My dad's hand shook as he ran it over my hair and forced me to look at him. The anguish in his eyes gutted me.

"I wish you'd told me," he said.

"I left to take care of Becca's sperm donor," Maui said. "And one of the others."

The way he said it, and the look in his eyes told me he'd discovered the truth I'd never allowed myself to believe. Seth hadn't been Becca's father. She didn't look anything like him, but she did share some traits with Dylan. I hadn't conceived her during the first time Seth and I were together like I'd always told myself. It had happened the night he and his friends raped me.

Still, even knowing the truth, he protected me, and didn't treat Becca any differently from before. He didn't care who'd donated to her DNA. As far as Maui was concerned, Becca was his and that was all that mattered. I didn't know how I'd gotten so lucky to find a man like him.

"They're all dead?" my dad asked.

"Two are. The other two will be soon," Maui said. "One is in prison, getting extra special treatment. The other is overseas. Casper VanHorne sent someone after him."

"Good. I want those fuckers burning in hell where they belong." My dad stood and leaned down to hug me. "And I'm so fucking sorry, Casey. I should have noticed something was wrong. I guess I didn't push because I was scared I'd lose you. We'd already been apart for seventeen years. I couldn't handle any more time away from you."

"I love you, Daddy. I'm sorry I kept this from you."

"I understand why you did." He kissed my cheek and left the room.

"You know the club may be told about it," Maui said. "I can't stop him if that's what he decides to do. You going to be okay if that happens?"

"I'll manage. I just don't want Becca to ever find out."

"She won't. I'll make sure of it." He kissed me softly. "Come on. Let's go check on our daughter. We'll have cake with our family, then I'm taking my girls home. I have a surprise for you."

As much as I'd loved what we'd done early this morning, I really hoped his surprise didn't have anything to do with sex. Otherwise, I'd need a heating pad or an ice bath to take care of any swelling.

Chapter Nine

Maui

I'd known Atilla would call Church, even before I received the text alert. He'd had a lot to process since our family dinner. While I didn't think he'd go into detail with everyone, he'd most likely make an example of me, which would mean telling the club at least some part of what Casey went through. Yes, I should have told him where I was going and what I was doing. If I'd gotten caught, he'd have been blindsided. But if I had to do it all over again, I wouldn't change anything.

I took my place at the table and waited for Atilla to call everyone to order. He hadn't spoken to me since I'd left his house. Even now, he wouldn't look my way. Either he was more pissed than I realized, or he couldn't see me without thinking about the fact I'd killed the men who raped his daughter. If something like that happened to Becca... it gutted me just thinking about it. I couldn't imagine how Atilla felt right now. I mean sure, hypothetically, I had an idea of how I'd react in his shoes. But without actually going through it, as a father, there was no way for me to truly understand.

"I didn't think we would have Church for another few weeks," General said. "Something going on?"

Rebel winked at me, which meant he thought this meeting was all about me claiming Casey. I had a feeling Atilla would bring that up, but he'd likely say something about my activity as well. Didn't matter that I was an officer of the club. If he felt I'd wronged him, or my brothers, he'd have to punish me in some way.

"I've called this meeting for several reasons. First, you all know Solena is due any day now. When the twins are born, I'm going to have Spade run things for that first week or two. I don't want Solena trying to juggle two newborns plus our other two kids all by herself. So if you need something, go to Spade first." Atilla glanced at me briefly. "Second order of business involves my daughter."

"Is Casey all right?" Truth asked.

"You suddenly care?" I asked. "Because you had a major attitude the last time we saw you."

"What attitude?" Atilla asked.

"He ran into us at the coffee shop. Casey and I had taken Becca to the park. When I said I was out with my family, Truth decided to run his mouth." It still pissed me off. I owed the fucker a punch to the jaw.

"I'm going to need more than that."

Rebel cleared his throat. "I was there too, Pres. Truth implied Casey tried to sucker Maui into believing the kid was his, or something to that effect. He nearly lost it when Maui called them his family."

"Well, for your information, they are his family." Atilla tapped his fingers on the table. "Casey only asked me for one thing on her birthday."

"What?" I asked, turning to face him. Was he seriously going to take that road? I couldn't even be angry about it. She'd been cute as hell telling her dad she wanted me.

"She asked for Maui. So I gave her my blessing and said she could have him." Atilla level me with a glare. "However, I didn't know at the time he was going to keep secrets from me."

I held my hands up in a gesture of peace. I didn't want to argue with him, and I sure the hell didn't want these men to know what Casey had been through. She'd never be able to look them in the eye again. Even if they didn't do it on purpose, they'd treat her differently. She'd notice, and then that night would continue to haunt her.

"Don't say anything, Pres. Please. Not for me, but for Casey. She's finally getting past it."

"Past what?" General asked.

I slumped in my seat, knowing Atilla would do or say whatever the fuck he wanted. I couldn't stop him. No one could. Except Casey, and she wasn't here.

"Some men hurt my little girl. Happened before she came here. It wasn't me she confided in but Maui. His little vacation time was spent killing the men who'd touched her."

Shit. He'd said enough. Now they'd know she'd been raped, and by more than one person. A loud *crack* made me jerk my gaze at the other end of the table. Truth had slammed his fist onto the table so hard, it literally split the wood in front of him.

"Are you saying I acted like an ass in front of a woman who'd…" I could hear his teeth grinding. The look he leveled at me told me how much he hated himself right then. "That's why you said Becca was yours."

"Since Casey is mine now, I'd have claimed Becca as my daughter regardless. I only ask that no one lets Casey know they're aware of her situation." I paused and tried to gather my thoughts. "If you look at her or treat her differently from before, she'll wonder why. Once she realizes you know what happened to her, it's going to hurt her. Badly. I killed those men so she can move on, so she won't have any more nightmares. Don't let it all have been in vain."

"Shit," Atilla muttered. "She was having nightmares?"

"It's why I asked you not to say anything. But you're a stubborn old goat," I muttered low enough only the other officers could hear me. "I assumed she hadn't been having them at your place."

He flipped me off then leaned back in his chair. "Apparently, I've fucked up, and I can admit as much. As Maui said, don't let Casey find out you know what happened. This is her home. Her safe place. I'd like to keep it that way. And for the record, no, she didn't have nightmares at my house. At least, not when I was around. I wonder if the stress from all the changes around here could have caused it."

That's the assumption I'd made as well. Since she hadn't said anything about those men reaching out to her, or seeing anything that triggered a memory, it had to have been stress.

"So she's going to need a property cut, right?" Rebel asked. "Or should we get Maui one that says *Property of Casey*."

My brothers nearly busted a gut laughing at my expense. I shook my head and let them have their fun. Hell, if she wanted to mark me as her property, I'd let her. I still had some room left for more ink. I could put her name on me. It was the one thing most tattoo artists warned against. Don't put someone's name on your body because you might break up. Except I knew I'd never let Casey go. She'd always be mine.

"I'll order a cut for her," Atilla said.

"Can you get a shirt for Becca?" I asked. "Something that shows she's my daughter?"

He smiled faintly and nodded. "I can do that."

My phone started to ring, and I quickly pulled it from my pocket. I should have silenced it, but I'd forgotten. Instead of turning it off, I stared at the screen.

"Pres, it's Wire. Can I take it?"

"Yeah. See what he wants," Atilla said.

I connected the call. "Do you have good news, Wire?"

"Lots of good news. Where should I start?" I put the call on speaker. Now that everyone knew, there wasn't any point in keeping the call to myself. "Oh, I know. Let's begin with Seth. I leaked the video of his confession, along with the buried files. News media outlets nationwide, and even a few overseas, have picked up the story."

"What about his family? Are they lying low?" I asked.

"His uncle, Governor Luton, is holed up in his mansion. His staff have said they will issue a press release later in the day. As for his parents, the father pulled a large amount of cash from the bank early this morning. After that, he got quiet. No idea where he is or what he's planning right now, but it wouldn't surprise me if he and the wife left the country. They have enough money to pull it off."

"And the other news?" I asked.

"Casper VanHorne called this morning. Parker is no longer an issue. His family will receive word sometime today that his remains were found at an underground brothel. Let's just say it's not the kind filled with women. Justice has been served, and no, he didn't accept his defeat gracefully. I was told you could hear his screams half a block away. Thankfully, the police don't really go to that area if they don't have to. Casper paid them to go retrieve the body."

Every man at the table winced and shifted in their seats. Looked like Parker got the same dose of medicine Chris was receiving in prison. Except his ended much sooner.

"Anything else?" I asked.

"Only one other thing. Well, it's more than one,

but they're tied together. I've wiped out any previous records Becca may have had. If anyone pulls her birth certificate now, medical files, or any other documents, it will show one Koa Akana is her father. Sorry to out your name like that, Maui, but I thought you'd be pleased to hear she's officially yours. Which leads me to part two. Congratulations! You're married to Casey. Although, you have my wife to thank for that one. While I was busy with Becca's files, she hacked into the local government and planted a marriage license and certificate for the two of you. There's really no stopping her once she sets her mind to something."

"Tell her I said thank you," I said. "Guess I owe my woman a ring now."

"Does she already know about her surprise?" Wire asked.

"No. How the fuck do you know about it? Then again, never mind. You've probably been all over my records, including my finances."

He laughed softly. "You're right, I have been. And you're welcome. I bounced the money from Seth's and Parker's accounts around multiple times, and through two offshore accounts, before depositing them into your account."

"Mine and not Casey's?" I asked.

"Lavender brought up that same question. I didn't want her to suddenly see a large amount of money. You can give her as much of it as you want, but I didn't think she'd want to necessarily know where it came from."

He made a good point. Atilla stared at the phone with a contemplative look. I waved it in his direction, wondering if he had something to ask the hacker. He leaned in closer.

"Wire, this is Atilla. You're on speaker, since Maui

never said anything. Are there more funds you can access?" Atilla asked.

"You mean from the other two men? Dylan didn't have two pennies to rub together, and Chris has been in prison for three months. Neither one was financially sound. However, Seth's father has three offshore accounts."

Atilla grunted and stared at the phone for another moment. "There's no way he didn't know what his son had been doing. You said you leaked files that had been covered up. I'm assuming by his parents?"

"Um, yeah. Sorry, I thought Maui had told you that part already."

"No." Atilla narrowed his gaze at me. "It seems there's still some pieces missing to what he and Casey have shared."

"Not my battle, so leave me out of it," Wire said "But yes, Seth's family did know what he'd been doing, and they tried to pay off anyone involved to keep their son's activities a secret. I will happily drain all three accounts. Where do you want me to send the funds?"

"How much is in each?" I asked.

"There's a few million in two of them. The third only has half a million."

"Only," Atilla muttered.

"Can you take the half million and donate it? Find a charity that helps women who've been raped, or maybe split the donation between a place like that and one for teen mothers? I think Casey would like that," I said.

"I can do that. In fact, I already do something similar whenever I take funds from assholes like these. And the other two accounts?" Wire asked.

"Do what you want with them, but I want one

million to be placed in an account for Becca. Set it up so she can't touch it until she's twenty-five. Hopefully, by then she'll have enough sense not to spend it all at once," Atilla said.

"How many kids are part of your club now?" Wire asked.

"I have two with twins due any day, and Lynx has twins he adopted. So between the two of us and Maui, there's seven. Why?" Atilla asked. "Or eight if you count Casey, but she's an adult now."

"How many are girls?" Wire asked.

"Aside from Becca and Casey, there are two other girls with a third on the way," Atilla said.

"For now, I need the names of the two girls already born. When your daughter arrives, send me her information as well," Wire said. "I'm going to put half a million into an account for each of them. While it might not seem fair to not include the boys, I think we can all agree if anyone should benefit from this money it should be the females. Besides, they'll be the most vulnerable."

Lynx and Atilla gave him the names of their daughters, and Wire said he was making a note to set up something for each of them, as well as putting a million aside for Becca. I only hoped my daughter never asked where the money came from, because I wouldn't tell her. She didn't need that hanging over her head.

"Maui, if I can make a suggestion, use some of that money to buy a new truck for yourself. I already know you're having an SUV delivered for Casey. In fact, it should be arriving any moment. You should also get her a ring, and maybe take your family on a nice vacation."

"Will you quit telling my men what to do?" Atilla

asked. Then he shot a look my way. "But he makes a good point. You need something better than Casey's car for transporting my grandbaby, and the three of you deserve to have some quiet time."

"Does that mean I get more time off?" I asked.

"Take a few days. A week tops," Atilla said.

"I'm going to take care of what I can on my end," Wire said. "And, Maui, you're welcome."

"For what? I mean, thanks for the info, and helping me take down those men, but I get the feeling you mean something else." Wire laughed and the call dropped. "What the fuck just happened?"

"Wire happened," Atilla said. "There's no telling what he's sending your way."

"Is he really giving my daughter half a million dollars?" Lynx asked.

"If he said he is, then you'd better count on it." Atilla smacked his hand on the table. "Church is dismissed, but I'd like Maui to hang back a second."

Everyone filed out, and I remained seated. Once the doors shut, Atilla leaned back in his chair and stared up at the ceiling. The man looked like he'd aged overnight.

"I can't punish you for what you did," he said. "Because if I do, it's like I'm punishing Casey. She's suffered enough already."

"You know she didn't want to tell you because she was trying to protect the both of you, right? Not only did she not want to relive those moments, but she knew you'd feel guilty for not being there to protect her. That was the last thing she wanted," I said.

"I know. Doesn't make that pill any easier to swallow. Instead of her protecting me, *I* should have been the one watching over *her*. I really hate her fucking grandparents for keeping us apart. They didn't want a dirty biker like me to be part of her life, and instead invited human traffickers in and let them take care of my daughter. How fucked up is that shit?"

"So we're good?" I asked.

"Yeah, we are." He smirked. "Son. You realize if Lavender married you to my daughter, that makes you my son-in-law, right?"

"Looks like I went from having no family left to inheriting a really big one. I got a wife and daughter, in-laws, and siblings."

"Welcome to the family." Atilla stood and patted my shoulder. "My girl seemed rather interested in your home state. Why don't you take the two of them there? Show them the beach?"

It wasn't a bad idea. "I'll see if I can set it up today. I'll text you the details when I have it all figured out. Just one little problem. Roscoe. Someone will have to take care of him while we're out of town."

"You still have that damn skunk?" Atilla asked.

"Yep. He's alive and doing well. Think Santiago would like to learn how to care for him? I could pay him twenty dollars for pet sitting while we're on vacation. He might like the responsibility of a job."

Atilla grunted. "Yeah, he might. I'll send him over later. You can introduce the two of them and see how it goes. If not, I guess I'll take care of the smelly critter."

I glared at him. "He doesn't smell."

Atilla gave me an *are you kidding me* look. I knew skunks weren't a normal pet for most people, but Roscoe was well-behaved, and he really didn't smell. In fact, pet ferrets smelled worse.

"I'm getting too old for this shit. I now understand why Grizzly, Cinder, and several others have retired." Atilla sighed and pinched the bridge of his nose.

I followed him out of Church and into the main

part of the clubhouse. "Sorry, Pres, but I think you're stuck with us for a while. Not one damn person here wants to take over your spot."

"Yeah, I know, and Santiago won't be big enough anytime soon."

He might grumble, but I knew Atilla loved being President of this club. Hell, we all loved being part of it. These men had been my family when I desperately needed one, and I knew it was the same for all of them. No matter what happened or what bombs life threw our way, we'd always have each other, and at the end of the day, that was more than enough.

Chapter Ten

Casey

I stood on the beach and closed my eyes, smiling as the breeze off the ocean ruffled my hair. If anyone had told me I'd one day be in Hawaii, I'd have laughed and called them crazy. I didn't know how Maui pulled it off, but he'd given me a dream vacation. Turning, I looked behind me where he sat under an umbrella with Becca. She'd enjoyed the sand, and now slept peacefully in his arms. He gave me a little wave and I made my way over to them.

We'd been here for two days already. Our first day, we'd met up with a local club, the Pacific Hawks MC, so Maui could pay his respects and let them know he was in their territory. They'd seemed nice and had been very welcoming. In fact, we were supposed to meet them for lunch today.

"Is it time to head in?" I asked.

"Yeah. We need to shower and get ready to go." He stood and I gathered our things. We walked up the dune toward the resort and rinsed off at the outdoor shower before going inside.

"Thank you for bringing us here. It's so beautiful," I said.

"I'm glad I can share part of my past with you. I know you wanted to see where I lived, but I'm going to have to decline your request. I talked to Kekoa. The crime in my old neighborhood has escalated over the years. There were over 60 rapes in the last year, and the population is under one thousand. I'm not risking you or Becca by taking you there."

I reached out to take his hand. "I understand and thank you for always protecting us."

"Are you going to be okay at lunch today? Only

the President and VP have old ladies. There might be other women there, but I can't promise they won't be club whores."

"Do you really think they'll have those types of women around their wives?" I asked.

"Never know. It's a small club. Hell, they may not even have club whores."

"You said we're going to the President's house, right? Wouldn't they have invited us to the clubhouse if they had one?"

"You're right. Although, since I'm here with my wife and daughter, they might have thought a family setting would be better. Guess we'll find out when we get there."

We stepped into our room, and Maui locked the door behind us. I went into the bathroom and started the shower. As much as I wanted to get clean, I knew I needed to bathe Becca before I laid her down. She could get in a short nap before it was time to go.

I went ahead and stripped out of my clothes while Maui undressed her, and took off her diaper, before passing her to me. I stood at the back of the shower and rocked Becca so the water would hit her briefly. Once I had her wet enough, I soaped her with baby wash, and quickly rinsed her off. She'd never had a shower before coming here and didn't care for them much.

Right as she started to fuss, I handed her off to Maui. While he took care of our little one, I washed off, making sure to clean the salt water from my hair. My skin felt tight, and I worried I might end up with a sunburn. My skin didn't look more than slightly pink right now, but by nightfall it could be a lot worse.

Maui was waiting for me with a towel when I got out, and he lightly patted me dry. "Someone needs some after sun lotion."

He smoothed it over my skin and gave me a soft kiss before stripping out of his swim trunks and getting into the shower. I stood on the bathmat, drooling over my sexy biker husband. If we hadn't had plans, I'd be in there with him. He smirked, clearly knowing the direction my thoughts had taken.

Later, he mouthed.

I wasn't sure what to wear. I'd packed for the beach and going on family outings. Since we'd be taking our rental car, it wasn't like I needed to be dressed for a motorcycle ride. Digging through my suitcase, I stared at the things I'd brought.

Maui came out of the bathroom with a towel wrapped around his waist and with another to dry his hair.

"It's just lunch with some bikers and their women." He kissed my cheek. "You're overthinking this. They know we're on vacation. Wear something comfortable."

He was right. At the same time, it was my first event to attend as his wife. I wanted to make a good impression. I selected a casual sundress and brown sandals. For little Becca, I chose the cutest outfit I'd packed for her. Once Maui had also dressed and combed his hair, it was time to head out.

"Do you know where we're going?" I asked.

"I know the general area. Once we get closer, I can put the address into my phone to pull up directions." He reached over to take my hand. "The house is probably going to be the size of ours, if not smaller, and most likely one level. But homes in Hawaii cost a lot more, so it's probably worth about two million."

My jaw dropped. "Are you serious?"

"Yep. Even the houses in my old neighborhood

probably run around six hundred thousand or more, and I told you what the neighborhood is like now. The nicer the area, and the larger the home, the more zeroes you need to add to the price."

"I knew it was expensive to vacation here. I guess it makes sense it costs a lot to live here too."

When we pulled up in front of the club President's house, it didn't look anything like I'd expected. A line of bikes out front told me we were definitely in the right place. The house looked like it had a makeover in the last few years. The outside was pristine, and very nicely landscaped. The houses at the Savage Raptors were cozy. This one was more like something I'd expect to see in a magazine.

"Looks like the club is doing well," Maui said.

"Apparently. I'm going to be too scared to set Becca down. What if she throws up on their floors or something?"

He shook his head at me and got out, unbuckling Becca from the baby seat in back. As he handed her to me, I looped my other arm through his and we went up to the front door. Maui knocked, and a pretty, older Hawaiian woman answered a few minutes later.

"You must be Maui and Casey. I'm Kapua."

"Kekoa's old lady?" Maui asked.

She nodded. "Yes, and his wife."

"Are there other wives?" I asked.

"One other. Come inside and I'll introduce you to Mahina. There are a few younger girls, probably a little older than you. Some of the men brought them as dates, thinking you might be more comfortable if we had more women present."

I smiled and followed her into the house. "That was really thoughtful. I'm used to not having a lot of women around. At home, it's just me and two others.

My dad recently got married, and one of the patched members is married."

"Are you the only one with a baby?" she asked.

"No. Lynx and Meredith adopted twins. My dad and Solena have two children with two more on the way. In fact, I'm surprised she hasn't delivered them yet."

"Your club is certainly growing." She smiled at me. "None of us have been blessed with children. Kekoa and I tried for years. I always miscarried. After the fourth time, he said it was too dangerous to keep trying and he had a vasectomy."

I reached out and placed my hand on her arm. "I'm so sorry, Kapua. I can only imagine how difficult that must have been for both of you. Does it bother you to have Becca here?"

"Not at all." She waved a hand. "It was long ago. I love little ones."

Maui held out Becca. "You can hold her if you want."

Kapua took her, cradling her close. She cooed to Becca as she led the way through the house to the back patio. Music played softly on a radio. I saw two coolers, and a table full of food. Kapua was right about the women. There were three who looked like they were in their twenties.

She took me around, introducing me to everyone, then made sure I had a cold drink. I watched as she carried Becca over to Kekoa. The big biker melted when Becca waved her chubby fist at him. I loved seeing her tame such big, tough men. One day she'd break someone's heart. Or have hers broken. Of course, anyone who hurt my baby would pay with their lives. I wouldn't have to lift a finger. Her daddy and grandpa would take care of it.

"You're Casey, is that what she said?" a blonde said. "I'm Marnie. I came here with Anela."

"Are the two of you dating?" I asked.

She laughed like I'd said the funniest thing ever. "No. Not in a million years. He's my brother's best friend. I'm only here as a favor."

"I'm Katie," said a redhead. "I came with Ahi. We aren't dating, but we've been friends for a few years now."

"And the other woman?" I asked. The brunette in question clung to another club member.

Katie rolled her eyes. "Lulu. I honestly don't know why she's here. She's chased after every biker on the island. Even those who aren't in a club. None of us can stand her, and she knows it."

In other words, she was the closest thing they had to a club whore, except I didn't know if the bikers actually slept with her. I wasn't sure how I felt about Becca being around her. She might be perfectly nice, but if these women didn't like her, I had my reservations.

"Why don't you fix a plate? We can sit and talk some more," Marnie said. "I doubt Kapua will be giving your baby back anytime soon. She adores children."

The ladies and I went to fill our plates and each grabbed a soda. We found three empty chairs near the fence and sat down. Maui stood near Kekoa, Kapua, and our daughter. He seemed to be enjoying his conversation with them. I wondered why he hadn't stayed in Hawaii and joined this club. How had he ended up with the Savage Raptors? Out of all the discussions we'd had, that hadn't been one of them.

"How long have the two of you been married?" Katie asked.

"We're actually newlyweds. When my dad asked what I wanted for my birthday, I told him I wanted Maui."

Marnie laughed until she cried. "That's hysterical! I love it."

"Who's your dad?" Katie asked.

"The President of the Savage Raptors."

Katie let out a low whistle. "My, oh my. You're the club princess."

I'd never thought of myself that way. It made sense, in a way. Perhaps if I'd grown up at the club, I might feel differently. Since I'd only been there a year, a lot of the time I still felt out of place. Which was odd since it was the only place I'd truly called home in my entire life. My grandparents hadn't been cruel to me, but I hadn't ever felt like I belonged with them either.

I spent another hour chatting with my new friends and kept an eye on Maui and Becca. I wished we had lunches like this back home. Maybe once more of the men settled down we could. Until then, I didn't think things would change much. For one, Solena was about to be completely exhausted. She already had two children at home and would soon have two infants.

I hoped we made it home before she went into labor. Even if I wasn't at the hospital with her, I wanted to support her and my dad. I was excited for the two of them, but I'd noticed the anxious way my dad watched Solena these days. He'd missed out on being present when I was born. Same for Santiago and Nora. This would be his first time watching his children come into the world.

"You ready to head back to the hotel?" Maui asked. "I think Becca is ready to take another nap."

"Sounds good. I think I'm a little worn out from all the sun today."

He leaned in closer to whisper in my ear. "I hope you aren't *too* tired."

My cheeks warmed. Well, I wasn't now. It didn't take long to get back to the hotel. Once I'd changed Becca into something more comfortable, I laid her in the crib. Within minutes, she was asleep. I ran my fingers over her hair, and marveled at how precious she was.

"Sweet dreams, my little angel."

Maui took my hand and led me into the bedroom. Our suite only had one, so we'd placed her crib in the living room. It was the only way we'd have privacy at night. She might be too small to understand what her mom and dad were doing, but it still made me uncomfortable to think of being intimate in front of her.

Maui closed the door and pulled me into his arms.

"Are you really tired? Because if you are, then I'll be content holding you while you sleep."

"I'm awake enough to take advantage of our daughter being asleep. If you still want to."

He reached for the hem of my dress and slowly lifted the garment over my head. "I more than want to."

It didn't take long to remove our clothes. Maui tugged me down onto the bed. Our legs tangled together as he wrapped my hair around his fingers, pulling my head back. His lips met mine, and I opened, letting him in. He deepened the kiss, and my nipples hardened.

"You're so beautiful," he murmured. "I'm a lucky bastard. You could have had anyone."

I shook my head. "No. There was only ever one choice. We're supposed to be together, Koa. There's no one else I'd ever want."

He kissed me again, then covered my body with his. I laced my fingers behind his neck, holding him to me. I felt his hard cock pressing against me. He'd barely touched me and I already wanted him. I arched against him, my nipples rubbing against his chest, and my clit pulsing with need.

Maui kissed his way down my neck and closed his lips around one of my nipples. He gave it a hard tug before scraping his teeth over it. It didn't hurt, but the slight sting made me want to beg. He released the hard tip and switched to the other side.

"Feels so good," I murmured.

"Not done yet." He worked his way down my body until he shoved my thighs farther apart with his shoulders and settled between them. He spread my pussy wide before swiping his tongue over my clit.

"Oh, God. Koa, please don't stop."

He licked and sucked until I'd come twice. With my legs trembling and my heart racing, I reached for him. I wanted to feel him inside me. No, I needed to.

He came up over me before flipping onto his back. With one arm, he hooked me around the waist and hauled me onto him.

"Ride me, baby. Let me watch you come."

His words made me feel hot all over. I eased down onto his cock, loving the way he stretched me. We hadn't tried it this way before, and I felt awkward as I lifted and lowered myself onto him. My movements weren't smooth or practiced. Was he even enjoying this?

I splayed my hands on his chest, feeling the thump of heartbeat under my fingers. Maui reached between us and played with my clit. I closed my eyes as pleasure rolled through me. Soon, I was moving without thinking about what I was doing. He pushed me closer to orgasm with every swipe of his fingers.

"That's it, baby. Come for me. Let me see how pretty you look when you're coming all over my cock."

I whimpered and my hips jerked. I rode him faster, and soon I was screaming out my release. Maui gripped my hips and surged upward, driving his cock up into me. It only took a few strokes before he came inside me.

I collapsed onto his chest and realized we'd never had that talk about babies. We'd meant to but hadn't gotten around to it. At the rate we were going, we'd be having another one whether we were ready or not.

"I love you," he said softly, running his fingers through my hair.

"I love you too." I kissed his chest before lifting my head and pressing my lips to his. "You're the best thing that ever happened to me."

"No, baby. You got that backward. I don't deserve an angel like you, but I will thank every deity known to man for as long as I live for you being mine. "

"We should rinse off then rest while we can. Becca will be up before long."

"Get up and I'll go start the shower. We can wash up together."

"Fine, as long as that's all you have in mind. I think I'm too worn out for anything else."

He winked as he got out of bed, and I had a feeling the shower was going to involve more than soap and water.

Chapter Eleven

Maui

Our trip to Hawaii hadn't lasted nearly long enough. We'd been gone four days, but they'd been pretty fucking great. I didn't know when we'd be able to go back. Even if we didn't go to Hawaii again, I'd love to take my little family to other places. Seeing the look of awe on her face when she saw the ocean for the first time was something I hoped to witness again. What other things did she want to experience? Before I'd come here, I'd traveled across the country. Ending up in Oklahoma hadn't been planned. I'd found the Savage Raptors when I needed a family the most. It had felt right to prospect for them, and eventually patch in. Now I was an officer for the club.

The furniture I'd ordered from Ravager was ready. He'd had our two Prospects bring it over, and they'd already placed it in Becca's room. It still felt unfinished. I'd have to convince Casey to help me pick out prints for the wall, or something to make the space look like a child's room.

Speaking of my wife and daughter, they were at Atilla's house. Solena wasn't feeling well, and I had a feeling it was nearly time for the babies to arrive. Casey had gone over to clean the house and cook a few meals for them. Atilla insisted he could handle it, but Casey didn't like feeling useless. So I'd taken the time to bring in a few more new items for Becca's room. It would be a nice surprise when Casey came home.

Roscoe kept pawing at my boots, wanting attention. When we'd first arrived back home, he'd been pissed at me and refused to acknowledge me at all. Now he wanted attention every second of the day. Finicky little shit. I reached down to scratch his back.

"Sorry I was gone for so long, buddy. But you and Santiago liked each other. I'm sure he took good care of you." Roscoe stared up at me. I'd take that as a skunk version of *so what*. He'd have to get used to it because I wanted to take Casey and Becca to more places they'd never been.

My phone buzzed with an incoming call and I answered without even checking the screen. "This is Maui."

"It's Wire. I thought you'd want to know I found Seth's parents. They're in Bryson Corners."

"What the fuck did you just say?" I asked.

"You heard me right. I have no idea why they're there. I'm hoping it's a coincidence, but it may not be. They probably know that's where Casey moved. I doubt they've tied her to their son's disappearance, and yes, he's technically a missing person since no body has been found."

"Never will be either," I said.

"I'm aware. Listen, if you can, keep Casey at the compound. They can't get to her there. I'm going to reach out to the local police. The father isn't exactly squeaky clean. Once they receive the information I have on him, I'm sure they'll arrest him."

"What the hell did he do?" I asked.

"Have you heard the saying the apple doesn't fall far from the tree? Seth's father has been covering up his own crimes for a really long-ass time. I'm slowly unraveling everything. Right now, I have enough for them to detain him. I'd love to have enough for them to lock the asshole up and throw away the key."

"What about the wife?" I asked.

"That's where things get really fucking bad. She's one of his victims. That asshole has been abusing her for decades. The really sick part is that she was only fourteen the first time he raped her, and he was in his twenties."

"Are you shitting me? How the hell did he get away with that? What about her parents?"

"Seth's family paid them off. The Lutons are a long line of monstrous men who do horrible things. The uncle is twisted in his own ways. I'll be blowing his life up pretty soon. By the time I'm finished, I'll have destroyed the entire family."

"Good. What do we do about the wife?" I asked.

"I'm going to find a safe place for her. Change her name. Give her money to start over. Whatever she wants, I'll see that she has it."

"If the husband is arrested here, then…"

"I believe Specter said he'd come visit you before he went home. He hasn't left Oklahoma yet. Once he finished with Seth, he took care of a few other things. He's in Bryson Corners now. Doubt he'll be able to keep his word about visiting the clubhouse, but he's agreed to get Mrs. Luton out of there and make sure she'll be okay."

"Wait, if that man has been with her since she was fourteen, then how old is she?"

"Nelly Luton gave birth to her only child, Seth, when she was fifteen years old. Since Seth and Casey went to school together… well, you do the math."

"Thirty-two. That woman is younger than me." Damn. I wondered if she mourned the loss of her son, or if she'd known he was just like his father.

"She'll get the help she needs. If she wants to fall in love and have another family, then she can. We'll make sure of it."

"Need anything from me, other than keeping Casey here?" I asked.

"No. I think we have it handled. Give your club a

heads-up for me? Just do it in a way Casey won't hear what's going on."

"I'll go talk to Atilla now."

I ended the call and grabbed the keys to my bike. Atilla's house wasn't far and I arrived in a few minutes. I parked beside Casey's new SUV, and then let myself into the house. Now that I was family, I'd been informed I didn't have to knock.

"Atilla," I called out.

"Kitchen," he yelled back.

I found him at the table with a beer in his hand, and my wife at the stove. It looked like she was still cooking. Now I just needed to get him to another part of the house, or outside. Somewhere Casey and Solena wouldn't hear us, or the kids.

"Got some club business I need to talk about," I said. It wasn't the truth, but I didn't know what else to say to get him out of here without my woman getting nosy.

"All right. We need the other officers or the rest of the club?" he asked.

"Wouldn't hurt to bring the officers in for this." The more of us who knew, the better.

"I'll have them meet us at the clubhouse."

I waited for him to make a few calls, then we got on our bikes and rode over to the clubhouse. We each grabbed a cold beer on the way to Church, where we knew we wouldn't be interrupted. Once everyone settled into their seats, I started to talk. I told them about the call from Wire, what he'd found out about Seth's parents, and about Specter being in our town.

"So what do we need to do?" General asked.

"Nothing, as far as I know. If they need help, I'm sure Wire will be in touch. For now, he said to let Specter handle Mrs. Luton, and he was reaching out to someone to have Mr. Luton arrested."

"An entire fucking family of rapists?" Spade shook his head. "Un-fucking-believable."

"From the sounds of it, the uncle was into other shit. But yeah, the entire family is rotten, and that poor woman was trapped in hell all this time," I said.

"I can't even imagine. They made her marry the man who raped her? Gave birth to his child, then her own son turned out to be just as evil as the dad. It's all kinds of fucked up," Knuckles said.

"How should we keep Casey on lockdown without letting her *know* she's on lockdown?" Atilla asked. "Because that girl is pretty sharp. She'll figure this out sooner or later."

"Not sure. I hope Wire makes his move soon. Once Mr. Luton is rotting in a cell, then it's safe for Casey to be out and about," I said.

Atilla was right, though. My wife was smart as hell, if I tried to delay her from leaving the compound, or found ways to keep her home, then she'd get suspicious. It wouldn't take long before she'd figure out we were keeping her here on purpose.

"So we tell her," General said. "If she knows it's dangerous to leave, she'll stay put. I know the two of you want to coddle her, protect her, and make her think the world is all rainbows and sunshine, but it's not."

"I don't want her to be scared," I admitted.

"She won't be," General said. "You took care of her problem before, right? So, it's likely she'll trust you to protect her now. Just be up-front."

I glanced at Atilla and he gave me a nod. While the officers kept drinking, I called Casey and asked her to meet me outside Atilla's house. It was one thing to tell her about Seth's parents, and another for Solena to hear it. If I put any stress on Atilla's pregnant wife, I knew he'd hand my ass to me. And I'd let him.

I pulled up and parked on the street, waiting for Casey to come down to me. She made her way across the yard and wrapped her arms around her waist.

"What's wrong?" she asked. "Did something bad happen?"

Very perceptive of her. "Got a call from someone about Seth's parents. His father is every bit as evil as Seth was, and for some reason, he's in Bryson Corners. I need you to stay at the compound until he's been taken into custody."

She paled and swayed. I reached out to grab her, pulling her across my bike. I needed her to be strong right now. This was why I hadn't wanted to say anything. I didn't like seeing the fear in her eyes.

"Mrs. Luton is a victim in all this. Someone is going to get her to a safe place and help her start over." I kissed her temple. "Everything is going to be fine, baby. Just stay close to home and don't go outside the gates until all this is over. It won't take long."

She nodded and cuddled against me. I wished we hadn't come back home yet. If we'd extended our vacation, then she wouldn't have been home for this mess. I knew we couldn't always run from trouble, and I didn't want to, but Casey had been through so much. She deserved a break, and some happiness.

"Where do you want to go on our next trip?" I asked. "You've seen the ocean now. Anywhere else you've always wanted to go?"

"Everywhere." She smiled up at me. "I'll go anywhere as long as I'm with you."

"Make a list of cities or states you want to see. We'll check them off one at a time. Maybe go somewhere twice a year. Sound like fun?"

"Yeah, it does. But can we afford to do that? And what about Roscoe? He's going to get depressed if we're always leaving him behind."

And now I needed to tell her the rest of what I'd kept from her. So, I confessed about the money, and everything Wire had discovered about the Lutons. I couldn't keep it from her. Not anymore. If it meant she'd be safe, then I'd do anything, even go against Atilla's wishes. Nothing meant more to me than Casey and Becca. Not even my own life.

"I love you," I told her. "More than anything in this world. You and Becca mean everything to me."

"I love you too." She pressed her lips to mine. "And thank you for telling me everything. I promise I won't leave the compound until you say it's safe. The last thing I want to do is run into Seth's dad. Still didn't answer my question about Roscoe, though."

I ran my finger down the bridge of her nose. "Good girl."

Her cheeks went pink. "Don't do that. Not here, not now."

Hmm. It looked like she'd enjoyed me calling her that. I'd have to remember that for later. "Are you finished here?"

"Almost. I'm just putting everything into containers and labeling it, with heating instructions. I'm sure Dad will be just as frazzled as Solena when the babies are here, so I'm trying to make things easier on them."

"You're such an angel." I hugged her tight. "I'm going to head home. Don't stay too long, okay? And as for Roscoe, we'll figure it out. You know I'll make sure he's taken care of anytime we're going to be gone for a day or longer."

"I won't. And maybe once Becca goes to sleep, you

can think of ways to keep me occupied at home."

"Are you trying to get pregnant?" I asked.

That sobered her. "No, but as much as we've been tempting fate, maybe we should just let it happen when the time is right. I wouldn't mind waiting until Becca is a little older, but if you happen to knock me up before then, maybe it's meant to be."

"All right." I kissed her once more, then helped her stand up. "Hurry home, baby."

I watched her go back into Atilla's house before I rode home. Let fate decide, huh? I grinned. Yeah, I could do that.

Epilogue

Casey

The last week had been completely insane. Police arrested Seth's father on multiple counts of rape, three counts of murder, embezzlement, and a bunch of other charges. He'd never get out of prison. Maui and my dad both assured me he'd suffer a great deal in prison. Apparently even inmates didn't like pedophiles, and Mr. Luton preferred raping young teenage girls.

Someone called Specter had gotten Mrs. Luton out of town and had tucked her away somewhere safe. At least, that's what we'd been told. I hoped she was okay. To think she'd suffered all these years. It made me sick to my stomach.

"You ready?" Maui asked, helping me from the SUV. He already had Becca, and I picked up the gift we'd brought with us.

"You think she's even awake? I'm sure the delivery was rough on her. She was in labor for hours."

"If she's not, we'll just take a peek at the babies and head out."

We went into the hospital and up to the maternity ward. I peered into the nursery, wondering if the twins might be there. I squealed and clapped my hands when I saw them. "Aren't they cute?"

"Yeah. Good thing they took after Solena." I smacked him in the stomach with the back of my hand. "I bet your dad is really damn proud right now."

"He should be. Look at them!" It reminded me of when Becca had been born. Hard to believe she'd been that small.

A hand came down on my shoulder and I looked up to see my dad gazing fondly at the twins. "She named them Constance and Ezra."

"They're beautiful, Daddy. And so small."

"That they are. But they're also damn lucky because they have two big sisters, a big brother, and an entire club to keep them safe. It's how I wish things had been for you when you were born."

I turned and gave him a hug. "Everything turned out fine, Daddy."

"Solena is asleep. Otherwise, I know she'd have wanted to see you."

I handed him the gift bag. "It's something for the twins, but there's also a few things in there for Solena."

"Appreciate it, honey, and I know she will too." He kissed my forehead. "Thank you for coming by. I think they're sending us home either late tomorrow or the day after. She bled a little more than they were comfortable with, so they want to keep an eye on her. Just to make sure everything's okay."

"Let us know if you need anything."

"I will. You take care of my sweet grandbaby, and all of you come over once we're home. I know Solena will want to see you and show off the twins."

Maui put his arm around my shoulders. "Maybe before too long you'll be coming up here to see us."

My dad narrowed his eyes at him. "Watch it, boy. That's my little girl you're talking about. Only way a baby is coming to your house is if the stork drops it off."

Maui snorted and I shook my head at their antics. I let them argue a bit more while I stared at my new siblings. He wasn't wrong, though. I might not be pregnant now, but sooner or later I would be. My husband couldn't keep his hands off me, and I felt the same about him.

Coming to the Savage Raptors a year ago was the best thing I could have done. I'd reconnected with the father I'd never known, fallen in love, and had the family I'd always wanted. To some, my life might not seem perfect, but to me it was. I couldn't have wished for a better father and husband than the ones I had.

Maui always said I was his world, but he was mine too.

I couldn't wait for the trips we'd take, the holidays we'd share, and all the memories we'd make together. We had our entire lives ahead of us, and I couldn't wait to see what the fates had in store for us. All of us.

Truth (Savage Raptors MC 4)
A Dixie Reapers Bad Boys Romance
Harley Wylde

Madison -- My parents died and left me with my older brother. At one time, he'd been a nice guy. Then he let drugs and alcohol destroy his life. Now I walk on eggshells every day, and hope for a way out of this nightmare. Growing up, no one wanted to be friends with the deaf girl, much less date her. Now I'm an adult and haven't been on a single date in my life. I should run from the big biker called Truth... so why does he make me feel so safe?

Truth -- Women are all the same. Can't trust them. I've been screwed over enough times to know better than to fall for the lies that drip from their lips like honey. But Madison doesn't seem to be the same as all the others. It's not just because she's deaf. There's a sweetness to her, a vulnerability that makes me want to protect her. I never thought I'd get the chance, but once I find out what her brother is up to, I'll stop at nothing to make sure no one hurts Madison. Whether she knows it or not, she's mine.

Prologue

Truth
The Past

Church wasn't the place to let my mind drift. I'd struggled to stay focused for the last month, and I knew my brothers were getting irritated with me. Instead of having a good excuse, I'd let some bitch get to me, and now I couldn't stop thinking about her. Didn't matter she'd run out on me. I'd believed her to be different. Then she'd disappeared without a word. Even though Jane hadn't been my official girlfriend, the club had known about her. It wasn't a secret I'd been seeing her. It also didn't mean I'd brought her around my brothers. Our relationship hadn't progressed to that point, and now it never would.

"As I mentioned, Bastard is still alive," Atilla said. "Except he's going by a new name. Garrison West. We have the Devil's Fury to thank for this tip. If it weren't for Outlaw's woman, Elena, we may have never discovered he'd survived. Since Bastard was one of ours, Outlaw reached out to me. They could handle this on their own, but this is our mess and we should lend a hand."

What? All right. *Now* he had my undivided attention. Looked like everyone else felt the same. Discovering one of our previous brothers was still alive, and doing some seriously fucked-up shit, was screwing with my head. There was also a rat amongst us, and the Pres hadn't yet said who it was. It really bothered me. Was the brother beside me the one who'd squealed, or was it someone else? I didn't know who to trust right now. I already knew I couldn't put my faith in women, but now my brothers too?

"How the fuck did he survive?" Rebel asked.

I wondered the same thing. He'd been burned, beaten, cut, and left for dead on the side of the road. By all rights, he should have bled out. We'd all assumed he'd died from his injuries. I hadn't gone to check, and I doubted anyone else had either. Now it was coming back to bite us in the ass.

"No clue, but he's still a piece of work. Now he's scamming churchgoers, with the help of a reverend. From what we've learned, he owns multiple brothels. Bastard is stealing the women, or luring them in with the promise of marriage, then dumping them in his businesses to turn a profit."

Atilla leaned back in his chair and pinched the bridge of his nose. What the hell else had he discovered? The look on his face made it seem like the weight of the world was on his shoulders. Did he blame himself for this fucked-up mess? Sure, if we'd made certain Bastard was good and dead back then, none of this would be happening. But still, it wasn't entirely our fault. Even though we'd known he was rotten, I didn't think any of us realized how bad it really was.

I might not trust women, but it didn't mean I wanted them to be used like that. I could only imagine the horror they'd felt when they'd realized what sort of situation they were in.

"Truth, I don't know how to tell you this, but... I was able to get a list of names from some of the brothels. It's something various hackers have been working on."

"Tell me what?" I asked.

"Jane's name is on the list. She didn't run out on you. Someone snatched her, then dumped her in one of those hell holes."

I stood so fast my chair fell over. "Which one?

How far? I can go and…"

Atilla lifted a hand, and it felt like a rock settled in my stomach. No. If he wasn't going to let me go after her, then…

"I'm sorry, brother. Jane's gone. She's one of many who committed suicide. She couldn't handle the things they made her do." Atilla dropped his gaze to the table. "We wouldn't even know this much if the brothels hadn't kept at least somewhat detailed records."

My chest felt tight, and I struggled to draw a breath. All this time I'd cursed her, thinking she'd left me. My Jane hadn't gone voluntarily. Someone had stolen her out from under my nose and made her live through hell. And what had I done? Nothing. I'd assumed she'd left of her own free will. I should have dug deeper, not given up on her.

I felt a hand on my shoulder and glanced at Rebel. He guided me back into my chair and I sat, feeling like my entire world had just imploded.

"What happened to her?" I asked, my voice seeming raspier than before.

"I'm not going to tell you that." Atilla stood and came over, putting his hands on my shoulders. "If you need a minute, we can take a short break. Take a walk. Get a beer. Whatever you need. I know this has to be a hard blow."

Jesus. If he wouldn't tell me what they'd done to her, then it had to be more horrific than even I could imagine, and I'd tortured my share of men. How scared had she been? Had she waited for me to come find her? I'd failed her and felt like a complete asshole for assuming she'd left me.

Atilla backed off and I stood, leaving the room. If he was going to give me a minute, I'd take it. I stormed out of the clubhouse and stood in the parking lot, just staring at the ground.

I hadn't been able to reach Jane for over a month. It had taken me about two weeks before I'd had enough and went to check her apartment, only to discover someone else had moved in. No one seemed to know where she'd gone, or when she'd left. For another two weeks, I'd kept trying to reach her by phone. I'd thought we had something good going, but when I'd discovered she was gone and she hadn't returned any of my calls, I'd assumed she was like every other woman in my life.

At seventeen, I'd caught my girlfriend cheating on me with my best friend. A few years later, I'd finally decided to give dating a try once more, only to discover the bitch was using me to pay her bills. She'd had multiple boyfriends. It had taken a while for me to give anyone a chance again, and when I did, Jane up and left without a word. I had shit luck with women, and I'd decided they were all traitorous bitches.

Which was why I found my mind wandering at the worst times. The Pres had already given me two warnings, so I'd tried to do better. I wasn't sure I wanted to find out what would happen when I had three strikes. And now, hearing she hadn't run out on me…

I felt so incredibly guilty, and beyond furious at Bastard. Hell, I was angry at myself and the club too. We should have put that fucker in the ground. If we'd hacked him to bits, there wouldn't have been any way for him to survive and go after Jane.

No. It hadn't been him. It was the rat. I needed to know who'd turned on this club and put their hands on Jane. I'd end that fucker, no matter what it took. I couldn't believe we had a traitor in our midst. The fact

I knew about it meant the Pres didn't suspect me. I wondered who else he'd told, or had he confronted everyone, hoping the culprit would give themselves away?

Once he gave up a name, I wanted just five minutes alone with the little rat who'd most likely been responsible for Jane disappearing. I'd make them suffer and beg for death. I couldn't imagine how Jane must have felt, or what she'd faced, in order for to take her own life.

Everything I'd known had been wrong.

I'd painted her with the same brush as every other woman I'd known. And look how it turned out.

I was better off alone. Women couldn't be trusted, but apparently I couldn't be either. I'd automatically assumed she'd proven herself to be like the others instead of realizing something was wrong. If I'd looked into her disappearance, could I have saved her?

I'm so fucking sorry, Jane. It's my fault. I hope you aren't suffering anymore.

I looked up at the sky, and wondered if she was looking down on me right now. Did she see what her death was doing to me? Did she want me to suffer the way she had? Or had she forgiven me in her last moments?

I'd never know, and that alone would haunt me the rest of my life.

Chapter One

Madison
Present Day

The stench from the house nearly made me gag. I'd often thought I couldn't keep living like this, but what other option did I have? I had the world's worst brother. He'd been a good kid, if a bit quiet. Now he was a total wreck. If his friends in high school hadn't convinced him to try drugs in the first place, he might have led a very different life. Would he even live long enough to see thirty? I couldn't remember the last time I'd seen him when he wasn't high or drunk off his ass. Since our parents were gone, it was just the two of us. If they hadn't left the house to him, I'd have thrown him out. As it was, I should be grateful he'd let me keep living at home. Since I'd been underage when they passed, I'd been left in my brother's care.

My brother being a piece of trash wasn't a big secret. Everyone in town knew about his problems. Hard not to when you lived in such a small place. And yet, he'd been granted custody without any issues. I wondered if it had more to do with the social workers having too many cases and not enough homes for all the kids. In their eyes, it was probably better to leave me with family than shove me into a house with four other foster kids and strangers for guardians. From what little I knew about being in the system, this probably had been the better choice. I'd heard some horror stories back in high school. No idea if any of it was true or not, but I hadn't been eager to find out firsthand.

The world could be a cruel place, especially if you weren't perfect. Because of my disability, I could have gotten into Section 8 housing, but the duplexes we had in town weren't any better than our house. In fact, they were in a much rougher area of Bryson Corners. Dealing with my brother had seemed like the safer option. Although, as I looked at the beer bottles strewn across the living room, the overflowing ashtrays, and his various drugs scattered on the coffee table, I had to wonder if living on the street wouldn't be better than this.

I didn't understand how he could afford his habits. He seldom worked, and when he did, he immediately drank his paycheck, smoked it, or snorted it. If it weren't for my part-time job working in the office of the local bakery, we wouldn't have electricity or water, and I would have certainly starved to death by now. Speaking of work… I looked at the clock on the wall and realized I was going to be late if I didn't leave right this second.

My brother slept on the couch, his mouth open, and one of his legs falling off the cushions. I didn't dare try to cover him with a blanket. Instead, I grabbed my purse and house key, then hurried out the front door. I locked up and started my walk to work. The bakery was nearly ten blocks from my house, but it could have been worse. At least I'd found something relatively close.

The sweltering heat left me sweaty and gross by the time I got to the bakery, but Mrs. Johnson merely waved as I rushed to the back. I could smell the bread she'd baked early in the morning, as well as the Danishes and other goodies. My stomach rumbled, reminding me I hadn't had time to eat breakfast. She allowed me as much coffee as I wanted, and a muffin or Danish each day as part of my employee perks.

I stashed my purse and stepped into the bathroom to freshen up. I splashed water on my face, used a wet paper towel to wipe down my arms and the back of my neck, then cleaned my armpits. Thankfully I kept a small bag stashed here with some deodorant and body spray. I used both before smoothing my hair and went to get a cup of coffee. I poured the strong brew and peered at the choices in the glass cabinet.

Mrs. Johnson caught my attention and signed her question. *What will it be this morning?*

I signed and spoke my answer, even though I knew my voice could be loud and off-putting to some people. "Blueberry."

She smiled and gave me a nod. Once she'd plated the muffin for me, I took my breakfast to the office and got started on my work. I paused between tasks to nibble on the muffin and take a swallow or two of coffee before getting back to it. I helped with her bookkeeping, inventory, and organized her files. As Mrs. Johnson once said, she loved the people and baking part of her business, but not so much the rest of it.

I couldn't call the vendors for her, but I did tackle the emails that came through, and I maintained her store website. In fact, I needed to go snap a few pictures for the shop's social media accounts. I grabbed my phone and peered out into the front of the shop. Only two men stood at the counter, both wearing the black leather vests of the local motorcycle club.

Even though they made me a little nervous, I pasted a smile on my face and stepped out front. Neither one acknowledged me, even though I did feel someone's eyes watching me as I took a few pictures. If it hadn't been for Mrs. Johnson's frantic waving, which I caught from the corner of my eye, the shouted *hey* would have scared the crap out of me. While it wasn't as loud to me as it would be for others, I still hadn't expected to hear someone speaking behind me. And for his voice to come through so clearly, I knew he'd yelled the word.

I paused and turned to face the men. One of them was speaking, but he was talking so fast, I couldn't catch everything. I had a hearing aid in one ear, which allowed me to hear a small amount. Still, I relied heavily on lip reading and sign language. Except this man's mouth was covered by a moustache and beard. I couldn't make out what he was saying. I tried to turn my hearing aid up a little.

"I'm sorry, I didn't hear you," I said. The man's eyebrows rose, and he came closer, moving slowly. Had he not realized I was deaf? I'd thought that was what Mrs. Johnson had been so frantic about.

"Why are you taking pictures?" he asked slowly, making sure to enunciate each word, and speaking loudly.

I showed him my phone, where I'd been in the process of loading a few images to Instagram for the Etta Mae's account. I turned so he could watch as I typed, added my hashtags, then posted the images. Next, I did the same for Facebook and Twitter. I'd save TikTok for another time, since I'd need to create a video of the items on display. I never liked doing that when people were present.

The other man came over and started signing. *He didn't mean to scare you. We didn't realize you couldn't hear.*

I signed my response back. *It's okay.*

"Can you say that out loud?" the first man asked. "I don't know how to use sign language."

"I said it's okay." The way Mrs. Johnson winced, I knew my volume had been a little too loud. "Sorry."

"I'm Truth," the man said. "And this is Knuckles."

The one he called Knuckles signed his answer as Truth spoke. So I did the same, both speaking and signing. "I'm Madison."

Knuckles patted Truth on the shoulder. They took their order from Mrs. Johnson and walked out without another word. But I did see the way Truth looked back at me over his shoulder as he approached his motorcycle. Butterflies swarmed in my stomach, and I wondered why they'd stopped to speak with me.

Mrs. Johnson caught my attention and started signing. *That was close. When you didn't respond, the man called Truth nearly lost it. He called you some ugly names and threatened you.*

My brow furrowed. Really? He hadn't seemed like the type to do something like that. Then again, anyone who'd met my brother before he'd become a junkie would have thought he was a sweet kid. As the saying went, you couldn't judge a book by its cover, and you most certainly couldn't judge people based on their looks. Truth's eyes had been intense, yet I hadn't sensed any hostility from him.

He seemed nice, I signed.

Mrs. Johnson shook her head and held her hands up, clearly done with the conversation. I felt the vibration of their motorcycles and watched as they drove down the street. Truth glanced my way one last time, and I'd have sworn he had a smile on his face.

I didn't know what to make of the man. Why had he called out to me? I paused and wondered if I should ask Mrs. Johnson. As much as she seemed to dislike him, I wasn't sure if she'd tell me. Shrugging it off, I went back to the office to finish the rest of my shift. When lunch rolled around, it was time to clock out and head home. I dreaded the idea of walking into the pigsty of a house, especially if my brother had finally woken up.

Mrs. Johnson had several customers, so I waved as I left the bakery. If I'd thought it was hot in the morning, I now felt like I might turn into a puddle before I'd even made it halfway home. Sweat drenched my clothes and plastered my hair to my head by the time I reached my house. I let myself in, and breathed a sigh of relief when I didn't see my brother. Of course, he could have just been elsewhere in the house, so I stayed alert.

He either woke up groggy and somewhat sweet, or mean as hell. There didn't seem to be an in-between with Justin. I went straight to my bedroom and put away my purse. As much as I wanted a shower, I needed to do something about the house first. I refused to live in a place that smelled like a trash dump.

In the kitchen, I pulled out the box of trash bags and placed it on the counter, knowing I'd need more than one. First, I collected the bottles in the living room and scoured the rest of the house to make sure he hadn't left some anywhere else. I dumped the bag into the outside trash can, before collecting the rest of the garbage around the house. Full ashtrays, food wrappers, a handful of empty soda cans. Every time I thought I was nearly done, I'd find more garbage. By the time I'd filled another two bags and deposited them into the bin outside, I still had to wipe down the coffee table, scrub the kitchen, and give the bathroom a thorough cleaning. We had to share one, and Justin had always been gross.

My back ached, and I felt ready to sleep for a month by the time I'd finished, but at least the house didn't smell awful and looked respectable again. Until he came home and trashed the place once more. Some days, I ignored it and hid in my room, unable to go through the intense cleaning spree every single day.

I checked the freezer and saw we still had some frozen chicken breasts left. I pulled out three and placed them in a pan of warm water to thaw a bit. Setting out a box of pasta, two jars of marinara sauce, a few seasonings, and making sure we had shredded cheese, I at least had figured out dinner for tonight. And possibly lunch tomorrow, if Justin didn't eat everything or bring home friends. More than once, he and his buddies had eaten all our food, leaving me with nothing even though I'd been the one to buy the groceries and cook the meal. I'd recently started keeping a few packs of ramen stashed in my room for emergencies. At least I only needed water to cook it, and since I paid the utility bills, I could guarantee I'd have at least that much to work with.

My stomach cramped and I knew I needed to eat something between now and then. Grabbing the bread from the cabinet, I slathered two pieces with butter, and quickly ate them, washing them down with a glass of water. It would take the chicken a little bit to thaw, so I went to take a shower.

I didn't plan to leave the house again, but I didn't feel comfortable going around in my pajamas, not when Justin and his friends could come in anytime. I picked out a pair of knit shorts and a soft tee before going into the bathroom and locking the door. When our parents had been alive, I'd enjoyed taking showers and relaxing under the hot spray. Not so much anymore. Now I tried to get clean as quickly as possible and get out. I couldn't trust Justin or the people he let into our house.

More than once, he'd been so high, he hadn't recognized me. I'd been terrified as he groped me, until my struggles and shouts finally got through to him.

He'd backed off, like he'd been doused in water. The second time, he'd passed out before he could do much. And the third, I'd thrown beer in his face. Of course, he'd wanted to kill me for wasting his beer, but at least he'd stopped what he was doing. Since then, I didn't feel safe in my own home. Even locking the doors still left me feeling uneasy. It wouldn't take much for a man to break through the flimsy locks. As thankful as I was to Mrs. Johnson for hiring me, the pay wasn't enough for me to move out on my own.

After I got dressed and combed out my hair, I opened the bathroom door and shrieked in surprise. A large figure loomed over me, and I took a hasty step back. My heart calmed its frantic pace when I saw it was Justin's best friend. Not that Ollie was an upstanding guy, but he'd never tried to hurt me. He was the best out of the guys Justin hung out with. Even when he got drunk or high, he still treated me like a kid sister, which was more than I could say for my own brother.

"Sorry," he mouthed, exaggerating the word.

"It's okay," I said.

He moved out of the way, and I went to the kitchen to check on dinner. Thankfully, I only saw Justin and Ollie in the house. As long as they didn't invite anyone else over, there would be enough food for me to eat too. I removed the chicken from the water, and realized while they weren't entirely thawed, it was enough they wouldn't flood the pan with a ton of water when the ice melted.

I preheated the oven and put the chicken into more hot water. When the oven flashed the correct temperature, I put the chicken breasts into a glass baking dish and slid it into the oven. Using the timer function on my fitness tracker, I set it for twenty minutes.

It had been a gift from Mrs. Johnson. While I didn't really exercise, I liked the fact it alerted me by vibrating on my wrist which meant I could set a timer to cook, and I'd feel it go off. I also used it for other things, and it was kind of fun to see how many steps I'd taken each day. If I had the money for it, I'd get one of those Apple smartwatches, but those were certainly out of my price range.

Justin stumbled into the kitchen and sloppily signed, *What's for dinner*?

I responded back in sign, *chicken parmesan. It won't be ready for about an hour*.

He turned and left, and I noticed Ollie watching from the doorway. "There's enough for all three of us. You can stay for dinner."

He flashed me a quick smile before following my brother. I wasn't sure if Ollie was the one who got my brother into this mess or not, but they were definitely in it together now. I only wished Justin could be more like his friend. At least Ollie treated me decently.

By the time dinner was done, all I wanted to do was eat and go curl up in bed with a book. We didn't have money to buy any, but I did sometimes go to the thrift store, and I'd catch a few on sale for only fifty cents or a dollar. I'd pick a few new ones and devour them within a day or two. My little shelf in my room had fifteen titles, and I'd read them all. Didn't matter. I'd read them over and over. It was my only escape from the misery of my life.

If the library had been closer, I'd have gone there to borrow books. For that matter, I'd have gladly sat there to read in peace and quiet for an hour or two a day. Unfortunately, it was too far for me to walk, and I couldn't drive there. Bryson Corners might not be the smallest town in the state, but we also didn't have public transportation. The only places I could go had to be close enough for me to walk.

Maybe one day things would change. Until then, I'd be content with my fifteen books, and if I was lucky, I'd be able to get another new one with my next paycheck. I mostly loved romances, but I also had a few mysteries and thrillers. Tonight, I wanted to re-read my favorite shifter romance. And if I compared the hero to the biker from before, well… no one but me would ever know.

Then again, with all that hair, he probably wouldn't be a wolf. No, he would be a bear shifter or maybe a lion. I smiled and started devouring every word on the page until my eyes grew too heavy and I had no choice but to sleep.

Chapter Two

Truth

"Glad to see you aren't always a dick," Knuckles said. "Good to know even you feel bad after yelling at a deaf woman."

"I thought she was being a stuck-up bitch and ignoring me. You know the women in this town either hate us or want to fuck us."

Knuckles winced. "I'd rather not put *all* the women into those two categories. The thought of an eighty-year-old grandma naked in my bed is enough to make me skip a few meals. Well, maybe not someone on par with Raquel Welch. That woman will be sexy no matter her age."

"Fine, smartass. All women under the age of sixty either hate us or want to fuck us," I amended.

"Better. Still not accurate, but I can live with it," Knuckles said. "You know, not all women are like the sluts at the clubhouse. You tend to bite off the head of every woman you meet. Except with Jane. You were different with her."

"Don't even go there," I said. "She wasn't the same as the others."

"Maybe the woman at the bakery is one of the good ones too. You won't know unless you give her a chance. I didn't see a ring on her finger."

"What are you? A fucking matchmaker?"

He flipped me off and I grinned at him. He wasn't entirely wrong, though. I hadn't given anyone a chance since Jane. The deaf woman wasn't stunning. In fact, I didn't know why I'd even noticed her. Her blonde hair was a warm honey color, and she'd been pretty enough, but she wasn't the type to make a man take a second look. Except... I had. At first, I'd been pissed, thinking she was a stuck-up bitch and ignoring me because I'm a biker. Then I'd realized she was deaf, and the way she'd looked at me had left me speechless. For the first time in my life, I'd suddenly wanted to protect someone.

Sure, I'd had the same thought about Jane, after I found out what happened to her. Up to that point, though, I had never felt like she needed me to watch over her. Madison might have a disability, but she seemed to do okay on her own. She had a job, and she'd been able to understand… wait. No, she hadn't. Knuckles had signed what I'd been saying.

"Why do you know sign language?" I asked.

"When I was a kid, there was a deaf boy who lived next door. I felt sorry for him because no one would bother to learn sign language, then made fun of him for not understanding when they spoke to him. So I learned how to speak with him."

"Who knew you had such a soft side?" I asked. He punched me in the shoulder, and I laughed at him, even though it hurt like a bitch! We didn't call him Knuckles for no reason.

Sign language, huh? I doubted it would be something I could pick up quickly. "How else could I communicate with someone who can't hear?"

"She has a hearing aid, so I think she can hear a little. Just speak slowly. And maybe trim up the forest on your face. I bet she reads lips, except no one could find yours right now."

I rolled my eyes at him. My beard wasn't *that* wild. Sure, I hadn't bothered grooming it lately. I could admit I did need to trim it a little, especially the hair covering my top lip. "I'll take care of it."

He grinned. "So does this mean you're going to go see her again? Maybe ask her out this time?"

"Let's not be too hasty. You said she wasn't wearing a ring, but we both know it doesn't mean she's necessarily single. I'll go buy some more muffins or something. Might take a few visits before I can figure out if she'd even be open to me seeing her outside her place of work."

Knuckles stared at me with his brow furrowed. "Where the hell did you put the real Truth? Because there's no way he'd ever say something like that about a woman. He'd just club her over the head and drag her off to his cave or push her against the nearest wall for a quick fuck, then move on."

"Like you said. Not all women are the same. I know the Pres and several others are tired of my shit when it comes to women. I'm sorry I don't immediately trust someone just because they have a pussy. I think we can agree women can be traitorous snakes."

Knuckles shrugged. "Some, but not all. And I think Madison is one of the sweet ones."

I took a swallow of my soda and bit into one of the cookies we'd picked up. Every now and then, someone from the club went by Etta Mae's to buy some sweets for the clubhouse. Today had been mine and Knuckles' turn. Had anyone else met Madison during one of their trips to the bakery? She'd come out from the back, and it looked like she handled things like their social media and maybe their website. Did she only do office work? Was that why I hadn't seen her there before?

"I don't know how old she is, but since Solena has lived here for a while and looks to be close to the same age, you could ask her about Madison," Knuckles said. "Get a little more info before you go back."

A hand slammed down on my shoulder. "What are we asking my wife about?"

I shrugged off Atilla's hand. "Knuckles thought she might know the young woman who works in the office at the bakery."

"Madison," Atilla said.

I turned to face him. What the fuck? "You know her?"

"I've seen her there before. Mrs. Johnson explained the girl works in the office and can't hear. That's pretty much all I know. But Knuckles is right. Solena may know more about her. Why?" Atilla eyed me. Yeah, I knew I had a bad rep when it came to women. He wouldn't let me forget it anytime soon either. "If you hurt that girl, I will personally bury your ass where no one will ever find you."

"Fucking hell, Pres. I'm not a complete asshole."

"But he did yell at her," Knuckles said. "And called her a few names."

I shot him a glare before focusing on Atilla again. "I thought she was ignoring me, until I found out she's deaf."

"He's sweet on her," Knuckles said, smirking.

I wanted to pound on the fucker to get him to shut up. I shifted on the barstool and couldn't deny what he said. It was true. I did like Madison, or at least what little I knew so far. One look into her eyes, and I'd wanted to put my arms around her and keep her safe from all the ugliness in the world. Which was something I'd never felt in my entire life before.

"I think she's nice, and there's something about her that drew me in," I admitted. Before the men in our club started settling down with families, I'd have never uttered those words. Things were different now. I knew Atilla would understand. Same for Lynx and Maui. Was that how they'd felt when they'd met their women? "I just wanted to find out more about her. She may not even be single."

Atilla folded his arms and studied me. I thought he was going to warn me away from her, but his next words shocked the hell out of me.

"Go back to the bakery tomorrow. Get a variety of cookies for the kids and stop by the house. You can ask Solena whatever you want in regard to Madison. But if she doesn't know anything, leave it at that. Don't pester her, Casey, or Meredith."

"All right, Pres. And thanks."

He grunted and walked off, heading to the back of the clubhouse. I finished my soda and stood, giving Knuckles a slap on the back. I had some work to do before morning came around. For one, I needed to trim my beard and possibly get a haircut. Second, I should come up with a plan, aside from bribing Solena for information on Madison. Something told me if things worked out with her, I'd have to fight the club for the right to keep her. To say I'd been a total dick would be an understatement. If anyone here deserved to find a good woman and settle down, it would be pretty much everyone except me.

Didn't help I still felt guilty as fuck over what happened to Jane. There was a chance she'd have ended up like all the others and proven herself to be a cheater, or to be using me in some way. Since she'd died, I'd never know. I also had to wonder if she'd have ended up in the brothel if I hadn't been dating her. Had they chosen her because of her connection to me? I'd never gotten any answers. As much as I'd wanted to beat the fuck out of Shepherd and get every detail out of him about Jane, he'd never given up his secrets. At least not when it came to Jane.

I got on my bike and headed home. I kept a small, sharp pair of scissors in the bathroom drawer for the times I wanted to keep myself from looking like Grizzly Adams. It had been a long time since I gave a shit about my looks. Women threw themselves at me whether I was an asshole or looked like I'd just crawled out of a cave for the first time in twenty years. The power of a Harley Davidson shouldn't be overlooked. The mere sound of the engine seemed to be enough to make panties drop. If that didn't do it, then my cut did. They liked the thrill of being with someone in a motorcycle club.

I parked my bike in the carport and went inside. Cleo greeted me with a soft meow and rubbed against my ankles.

"Hey, girl. How's my sweetheart?" I asked, leaning down to scratch her ear. I picked her up and cradled her against my chest. I'd found her six months ago. Some asshole had beaten her, popped her eyeball, and cut her up pretty bad. The vet hadn't been sure she'd make it. If I hadn't heard her pitiful cries, she'd have died amongst the trash in an alley. Now my sweet girl had one eye sewn shut and they'd had to remove one of her front legs.

She purred and cuddled against me as I carried her back to my room. I placed her on the bed, where she immediately curled up and closed her eye. Even after all these months, she still became anxious when I left the house. The vet said that red tabby females weren't common. They'd called her a boy when I'd first walked in holding her. Once I'd gotten to know her better, I'd named her Cleo, short for Cleopatra, because the girl acted like a queen once she'd settled in a bit.

In the bathroom, I pulled out my beard comb and the scissors. Combing my moustache down, I tightened my upper lip and carefully trimmed the hair. It took a few times of combing and trimming before I had it even and a length I thought would be good for Madison to be able to read my lips. I went ahead and combed out the rest of my beard and realized the entire thing needed to be cleaned up. I kept trimmers under my sink, but if I was going to get a haircut anyway, I might as well ask the barber to handle it.

The next time I saw Madison, I wanted to be able to talk to her without needing someone's help. Which meant I also needed to look up some videos on basic sign language. Until I knew if this was going to work between us, I wouldn't entirely immerse myself in it, but it wouldn't hurt to learn a few things. There was a chance I might need the skill at some point.

"Jesus. I barely spoke to her, so why the hell is my heart racing at the mere thought of seeing her again?" I stared at my reflection. What had she thought about me? She hadn't seemed scared. Of course, I hadn't exactly seen desire in her eyes either. More like curiosity. I could live with that, for now.

I stopped long enough to give Cleo a kiss on top of her head, then went back outside to my bike. The barber wasn't too far away, and he allowed walk-ins. I only had to hope the place wasn't packed. If there was one thing I hated more than catty ass bitches it was having to wait for an hour or more -- for any reason. I didn't do long waits for food, haircuts, or even medical appointments. Life was too short to spend it sitting on your ass waiting for something.

By the time I'd gotten my hair and beard trimmed, my stomach was rumbling. I stopped at a burger place before heading home. Cleo would be pissed I didn't get her anything, but the vet made it clear fast food was bad for her. Instead, I paid a mint for her expensive ass kibble and treats, all approved by her doctor. My little queen had to be the most spoiled kitty in Bryson Corners. She had two cat trees, and so many damn toys I was always stepping on them. At least, I had until I'd figured out how smart she was. Now Cleo had a toy box and she literally picked up her toys and put them away.

Until her, I'd never realized cats were capable of something like that. If my brothers knew I scrolled through TikTok to watch cat videos, they'd give me shit for the rest of my life. It had been the place where I'd gotten the idea for the toy box. Although, I hadn't expected her to pick them up herself.

My phone rang right as I pulled into my carport, and I turned off the bike before answering.

"This is Truth," I said when it connected.

"You need to head over to Murphy's, and I mean right the fuck now," Knuckles said.

"Why? We have perfectly good beer at the clubhouse. Why would I want to go to that shithole?"

"Because your girl is there, and it looks like she's in some serious trouble. I'm banned so I can't go inside. Some guy pulled up in a clunker, hauled her out of the passenger seat, and dragged her inside. I think she's drugged, Truth."

"Son of a bitch," I muttered. "I'm on my way. Don't let anyone leave with her."

"I'll stay and watch the place."

I backed down the driveway, and flew down the street inside the compound, not even slowing as I approached the gates. If the Prospect hadn't opened it fast enough, I'd have driven right through the damn thing. The second I hit the main road, I shifted gears and opened up the bike, eating up the pavement at more than thirty miles over the speed limit. I dared a fucker to pull me over right now.

I might not know Madison, but I'd be damned if I'd let anyone hurt her. Whoever had her, they'd better have their affairs in order. By the time I finished with the fucker, he'd be lucky to be alive. Fury filled me at the thought of her being drugged and helpless. Everyone knew what went down at Murphy's. The cops hadn't shut the place down due to lack of evidence, but it didn't mean bad shit didn't happen. The owner was just good at keeping all the trash hidden from public view. A bouncer at the door wouldn't let in anyone who didn't look like they belonged there.

I skidded to a stop in the parking lot, put down the kickstand, and shut off the bike. I saw Knuckles in the shadows but didn't acknowledge him. The bouncer at the door took one look at me and stepped out of the way. I barreled inside, ready to slaughter anyone who dared to hurt Madison.

It only took me ten seconds to find her. The greasy motherfucker holding onto her was dangerously close to getting a one-way ticket to hell.

I stomped over toward the table and glared at where he had his arm around her shoulders. The glassy gaze she lifted to mine made me growl. Fisting my hands, I took a breath and tried to rein in the rage I felt.

"Can I help you?" one of the other men at the table asked.

"Yeah. I'm here for my girlfriend, and she better not have so much as a bruise or scratch on her. Otherwise, every man at this table is about to have a very bad night."

The one with his arm around her frowned. "What the hell are you talking about?"

I held my hand out to Madison. "Come on, honey.

Let's go."

She gave me a big smile and placed her hand in mine, only for the man to yank her closer to him.

"Look, buddy. My sister doesn't have a boyfriend. I don't know what you're playing at, but you need to leave."

Sister? My gaze shot from him to her and back again. There were a few similarities. The fact he would do something like this to his own flesh and blood only made matters worse. What had she suffered up to this point?

"I'm not asking you. I'm *telling* you. Madison is coming with me. Now get your hands off my woman before I decide Murphy's needs new décor."

"What does that mean?" the brother frowned.

"It means the walls and floors will be covered in the blood of every asshole at this table." I braced my hands on the scarred wood and leaned in closer to him, making sure to catch the gaze of all three men. "Do you think I'm lying? Think I can't take out all three of you without breaking a sweat?"

One of them held up his hands. "I don't care what you do with her. Justin here was just offering her up as partial payment for what he owes us. But honestly, pussy is pussy. Nothing special about the girl."

"I'm sorry. He was doing what?" I asked.

The guy smirked. "You heard me."

I felt someone at my back and looked over my shoulder. Rebel gave me a slight nod. I didn't know when he'd arrived, or how he'd known I'd need help, but I was grateful for the backup. Maybe Knuckles had called him.

I nearly tore Madison away from her brother and thrust her at Rebel before fisting Justin's shirt. I hauled the fucker out of the booth and slammed my fist into his face. His nose broke and blood ran down over his lips. I didn't stop with one blow. I pounded the fucker until you couldn't recognize him anymore, then kicked him in the ribs twice for good measure. My chest heaved with every breath, and still I wanted to keep going. If I didn't worry about Madison remembering all this later, I'd have killed the bastard right here and now.

I spat on him and glared at the men. "Whatever he owes you, Madison has nothing to do with it. I even hear someone has been sniffing around her, or thinks of taking her as payment, and I will gut every last one of you motherfuckers. Am I clear?"

"Take her. We'll make other arrangements with Justin. Assuming he survives the beating you just gave him." I made sure to memorize each man's face, but especially this one. He seemed to be in charge.

"How much does he owe?" I asked.

"Ten grand, but interest is accruing every day." The man shrugged. "It's business, nothing more."

"If he dies, I'll pay the debt. Keep Madison out of this shit."

"You have my word. None of my men will hurt her."

Something about the way he said that set me on edge. None of *his* men. Did it mean the shitty brother owed money to other people? Would they come for Madison at some point? I'd deal with it later. For now, I needed to get her the fuck out of here.

I turned my back on them, stepped on Justin's nuts on my way to the door where Rebel stood with Madison, and then took my woman in my arms. I carried her out to my bike and wondered what the hell I'd do with her now.

"I don't think she can ride," Knuckles said. "It's

why I called Rebel. He brought one of the club trucks."

I hesitated a second, then handed my keys to Rebel. "Take my bike to my house. I'll drive Madison."

Knuckles smirked and I flipped him off. I was only doing it so Madison wouldn't be with a man she'd never met. At least, that's what I told myself. If I'd been honest, I'd have admitted I didn't like the idea of her riding with anyone else.

Something told me things were about to get interesting.

Chapter Three

Madison

My head pounded and I groaned as I pressed my hand to my forehead. What the hell happened? I remembered having dinner with Justin and Ollie, then… nothing. I rubbed my eyes, trying to clear my vision. A quick touch of my ear and I realized I still had my hearing aid in. I quickly removed it, anxious I may have damaged the device. It wasn't the type I really needed, but it had been the only one insurance would cover.

I shrieked when a man's face loomed in front of me. Scrambling back against the headboard, I pressed a hand to my chest as my heart raced out of control. Then I realized who he was. Truth.

"You scared me," I said. He didn't exactly wince, but I could tell from his expression I'd been incredibly loud. I put my hearing aid back in. "Sorry."

"Stop apologizing," he said slowly, and I noticed he'd trimmed his beard so I could read his lips.

"Where am I?"

"My house," he said. He held up a finger and left the room only to return a few minutes later with a notebook and pen. He held it up and I read the message. *Your brother drugged you and took you to a bar last night. Do you remember?*

What? Justin had done that? More importantly, how did Truth know? I shook my head, and he started to write something else.

Are you aware he's a drug addict who owes money to some unsavory people?

Unsavory? I smiled, liking the fact he'd used the word. Most would have called them bad people. Not Truth. Then I immediately sobered. Why had Justin done it? He'd never tried something like that before. Even if I'd been drugged, if he'd let someone hurt me, I'd have felt it the next day. Wouldn't I?

"I know he's an addict. He started using in high school."

He thumped the pen against the notebook before writing again. *He tried to use you as a way to reduce his debt. Do you understand*?

While yes, I did know what he meant, I tried to convince myself he had to be wrong. Justin wouldn't do that to me. Except, I knew my brother wasn't the same person he'd been before the drugs and alcohol. The addict very well might try to sell or trade me to get what he wanted, or to save his own ass.

He started writing again. *You can't go home. It's not safe*.

"You know I live with my brother?" I asked.

His lips pressed into a tight line, and he furiously wrote on the paper. *I do now. You definitely aren't going back there*.

I glared at him. "Why do you get a say in it?"

He smirked. *Because I told everyone in the bar you're mine*.

My cheeks warmed and I couldn't hold his gaze. His? No one had ever wanted to date me in school, or since then. Now this big, sexy biker said I belonged to him? I wasn't sure what to think or how to feel. He'd fascinated me in the bakery, and I'd thought of him even while I'd been reading.

I sucked in a sharp breath. "I'd been reading in bed. That's the last thing I remember."

I'm not sure how he drugged you, or when. I only know you had glassy eyes and looked high when I brought you home.

Justin had really done such a thing to me? Had he

injected me with something while I slept? Or had he slipped something into my food or drink when I wasn't looking? I felt betrayed and violated. As much as I hated to admit it, Truth was right. It wasn't safe for me to go home. Where else could I go? If I'd had any other options, I'd have used them by now.

I felt a gentle touch on my chin and looked at Truth. The concern in his eyes eased some of my tension. When was the last time I'd had someone worry about me? Probably not since my parents died.

"You're going to stay here," he said. "I'm not asking. I'm telling you."

He spoke slowly enough I could read his lips, and my stomach flipped when I realized what he'd said. He couldn't mean he wanted me to move in permanently, right? What sort of insane person would do something like that?

"I don't understand," I said.

He picked up the pad and pen again. *I told them you were my girlfriend. Your brother argued and said you didn't have a boyfriend. We need everyone associated with your brother to believe what I said. What kind of boyfriend would send his sweet girlfriend back into hell with a brother who tried to trade her in order to lessen a debt*?

When I read what he wrote, I understood his reasoning, even if I didn't like it. Even though I'd considered him insane for wanting to keep me here, a stranger he'd just met, I had to admit I felt a little disappointed by his reasoning. Although Mrs. Johnson said he'd called me names, I'd thought he was a good man, and he was proving me right.

But I needed to know what she'd meant. "Mrs. Johnson said you called me names and were angry when we met."

He winced. "I'm sorry."

I waited. Clearly, it was an admission he'd done that very thing, but I didn't understand why. We'd never met before. What could I have possibly done to make him so angry? Or was he like that with everyone?

He started writing again. *I thought you were ignoring me when I was speaking to you. Mrs. Johnson said you hadn't heard me, so I shouted louder, not realizing you were deaf. I'm sorry for doing that.*

I nodded, accepting his apology. I couldn't imagine what would make him react in such a way, simply because he thought someone wasn't paying attention to him. Did he have some sort of trauma in his past? I had a physical disability, but I knew sometimes emotional scars ran much deeper than ones you could see. For now, I'd give him the benefit of the doubt. Until he proved he deserved me to be upset with him or feel offended by his actions, I'd put my faith in him. As of right now, the man was my savior. He'd rescued me last night, even though it wasn't his job to do so. He may have told everyone I was his girlfriend, but we both knew the truth. We'd met one time, and very briefly.

"I need my things," I said.

"I'll ask Knuckles to go with us. You can pack anything you want to keep. We'll take one of the club trucks." He ran the backs of his fingers down my cheek. "We'll keep you safe."

Did he have room for all my things? The only items that truly belonged to me were in my bedroom, and my bathroom items. Everything else went with the house, which meant they technically were my brother's property. My stomach knotted at the thought of him keeping all our parents' belongings. I didn't think he'd miss a few pictures, though. I could at least keep those to remember the times when things were better.

"Why are you helping me?" I asked. "You don't know me."

He smiled faintly, then picked up the pen once more. *Because I'd hoped we'd get a chance to know one another better. I'd planned to visit the bakery again this morning so we could talk more.*

Really? I held his gaze and saw he meant what he'd said, or rather written. It felt like butterflies were swooping around in my stomach, and I knew this man would be far more dangerous to me than my brother. For the first time in my life, he was giving me hope. I'd always thought no one would want a defective woman like me. Truth was proving me wrong.

Oh no! The bakery! My eyes widened and I frantically searched for my phone. Even though I couldn't call Mrs. Johnson, I could at least text her.

"What's wrong?" Truth asked.

"I'm late for work."

He shook his head, smiling again. Pulling out his phone, he showed me he was calling the bakery. I couldn't catch everything he said to Mrs. Johnson. It didn't really matter. The fact I had someone helping me, trying to support me, left me feeling a bit like the world was shifting under me. I'd never felt so off-balance before. Where had this man been all my life? Then again, he looked quite a bit older than me. Maybe I hadn't noticed him before because he'd never made his presence known to me. If he hadn't yelled behind me in the bakery yesterday, we'd have never spoken.

Mrs. Johnson might have been upset over what he'd said, but it had led to a conversation between us. Without that interaction, would he have run off to rescue me last night? Probably not. I wasn't sure anyone would have even bothered calling him.

Knuckles wouldn't have had any idea who I was, so he wouldn't have noticed me at the bar. I firmly believed things happened for a reason, even my deafness. I'd been born with total hearing loss in one ear, and what they considered profound hearing loss in the other. My hearing aid enabled me to manage better than someone who was completely deaf, but not enough to communicate like a hearing person.

When he ended the call, he reached over to take my hand. I linked our fingers together, holding onto him like a lifeline. And I realized he was, at least for me right now. Without Truth, something horrible would have happened to me. I might very well have disappeared without a trace. I owed him so much.

"Thank you," I said. "For everything."

"I've done a lot of fucked-up shit in my life, Madison. But one thing I will never condone is someone hurting an innocent woman."

I smiled a little. "Only the bad women?"

He shrugged and didn't respond. I wasn't an idiot. I knew women could be every bit as deadly or mean as a man could. While it wasn't common for a serial killer to be a woman, there was a reason that percentage wasn't a big fat goose egg. Because there were some. At least I knew he considered me to be one of the good women, and it also gave me another clue about why he'd yelled at me. Someone had hurt Truth at some point. Might have been more than one woman. Before I could second-guess myself, I reached out and hugged him. I felt the steady *thump* of his heart against me, and the warmth of his hand where it pressed against my back.

Drawing back, I swallowed hard as I held his gaze. Why did this man make me feel so many things, and so strongly? I'd never met anyone like him before. Was this what people meant when they said they'd fallen in love at first sight? I didn't consider myself in love with him. I might like reading books with happy endings, but even I didn't believe in fairy tales anymore. Still… there was certainly something about him. A pull that made me want to stay by his side as long as he'd allow it.

Yeah… this man was definitely more dangerous than my brother. At least with Justin, I had a chance of escaping unscathed. But Truth? He had the ability to completely wreck me, and I didn't think he even realized it.

"Come on. I'll make some breakfast for us, then I'll call Knuckles and we'll go pack your things. Mrs. Johnson said not to worry about coming in today, tomorrow, or the day after."

Even though he'd spoken slowly, I'd only caught bits and pieces, but enough to put it all together. So I had some time off? While I should be excited, I could only think about how much money I'd be losing. I didn't make much to begin with. Of course, if I wasn't living with Justin anymore, I didn't have to worry about stocking the kitchen or paying the utilities. Then again, I didn't think Truth was going to let me live here for free either. We'd have to sort everything out.

I followed him to the kitchen and sat at the table while he started pulling things out of the fridge. Looked like he was going to make biscuits with bacon. No one had cooked for me since my mom died. It was nice getting to sit and not worry about feeding myself or my brother. While everything cooked, I remained silent. There wasn't much point in talking to him, when I wouldn't be able to read his lips, and he couldn't very well write out what he was saying while he flipped bacon.

I took the time to look around his kitchen. The walls were the color of butter, which brightened up the room. The table wasn't overly large but would seat four people. Did he have company over often? I wondered if he sat at this table to play cards with his friends, or if he'd brought girlfriends here and cooked for them like he was doing for me now.

Something brushed against my ankle, startling me. I looked down and saw an orange cat weaving around my legs. Truth didn't seem like the sort of man to own a cat. Bending down, I scratched behind its ear. Poor thing was missing an eye and a leg. Maybe Truth had a soft spot for anyone in trouble, be they human or animal.

He slid a plate in front of me with three biscuits and way too much bacon on it, then placed some juice beside it. I smiled my thanks and immediately pulled the biscuits open. Before he'd had a chance to put butter and jelly on the table, I'd broken up my bacon and stuffed it inside the biscuits. I'd done this so many times when I'd been younger.

"That's Cleo," he said. "As you've seen, she's very friendly."

I took a bite of food, "It's good. Thank you for breakfast."

He winked and dug into his food. I noticed he was texting as he ate and wondered if he was talking to Knuckles. He'd mentioned asking him to come along with us. Probably because I already knew him, and the man could sign. Would Truth be willing to learn? It would certainly make it easier to speak with him. Then again, this was probably just a temporary thing. He might have said he was interested in learning more about me, but that didn't mean we'd get a happy ending.

I needed to keep myself grounded in reality. If I started daydreaming about a wedding and kids, then I'd most likely end up disappointed. Besides, did guys like him even get married? I knew a few had women and kids, but that didn't mean they believed in saying their vows and making it legal. I had so many questions. Would he be offended if I asked them? *Slow down, Madison. You can ask him stuff without blurting it all out at once.*

Right. I'd take my time. He wanted us to get to know one another, so that would be a good way to do it. I'd answer his questions, and he could answer mine. I smiled, feeling excited about the thought of having a boyfriend. We were only pretending. I knew that. It didn't mean things couldn't change, though. There was a chance I'd be his girlfriend for real one day.

"Knuckles will be here soon," he said. "I have a toothbrush you can use."

I stood and followed him back to his room and into the bathroom. He opened a drawer filled with new toothbrushes. My eyebrows rose as I stared at them. He tapped me on the shoulder to get my attention before speaking.

"I tend to buy necessities in bulk. This doesn't mean I've had a ton of women in my house. In fact, you're the first in a long time."

I nodded, oddly pleased with that knowledge. I selected a toothbrush, and quickly cleaned my teeth. When we went outside, Truth helped me into a truck parked in the driveway, and I saw Knuckles on his motorcycle out on the street. The biker joined us, getting into the back seat next to a biker I didn't know. His patch said his name was Rebel. I hadn't even realized someone was already inside the vehicle.

Part of me really hoped Justin wasn't home. And

the other part… well, it would be nice for him to see I had people protecting me now. Of course, he'd already know that if Truth took me away from him last night.

I told him my address and watched the scenery pass as Truth drove. When we got to the only place I'd ever called home, my throat grew tight. Would I ever come back here again? Or would this be the last time I ever stepped foot inside my childhood home?

It was a bittersweet feeling. This place had been hell on earth since my parents died, and yet, it was still home.

Whether I was ready or not, it was time to face a new chapter in my life. I only hoped it went better than the last one. I wasn't sure how much more I could handle.

Chapter Four

Truth

I stared at the house. The neighborhood wasn't terrible. In fact, every other house on the street seemed to be in good shape. This one, however, hadn't received proper care for a while. The lawn looked wild and had weeds growing everywhere, sections of the paint had chipped off the house, and the concrete pad in front of the door had many cracks. Weeds even sprouted along the walkway, sticking up through the center of the cement path.

Madison's hand trembled as she reached out to turn the knob. It gave easily, which meant her brother hadn't bothered to lock it. I didn't see a car in the driveway or out in front of the house on the street, so I didn't think her brother was here. Considering the sorts of men he'd been with last night, I didn't like the idea of Madison entering the house first. I placed my hand on her arm and gave Knuckles a nod to sign as I spoke.

"Honey, you need to wait a minute and let me clear the house. What if someone is hiding inside, just waiting for you to come home? You could get hurt."

She bit down on her lip and gave a slight nod before taking a step back. Knuckles placed himself in front of Madison, while Rebel stood behind her. I pulled a gun from the holster at the small of my back and entered the house, weapon outstretched in front of me as I went room by room. After every closet, underneath each bed, and any other potential hiding spots had been checked, I put my gun away and went back to the front door.

"House is clear," I said. I didn't mention the mess inside. Something told me Madison hadn't left it like this.

Knuckles entered with Madison behind him, and Rebel bringing up the rear. The resignation in Madison's eyes told me it wasn't the first time she'd walked into this particular sight. Did her brother always trash the place?

I lightly touched Madison's hand to get her attention. Knuckles moved beside me and signed for me. "What do you need to pack? Just your room, or do you need things from the rest of the house?"

"Everything belongs to my brother. My parents left him everything," she said.

Stubborn girl. "Not what I asked. You can take anything you want, Madison. Your brother isn't going to stop you, and he can't very well call the police. If he did, he'd risk getting arrested for possession. Now, tell me what needs to go with us."

The tension left her, and she gave me a slight smile. "I want some pictures, my mother's favorite baking dish, and the recipe book she inherited from my grandmother. And everything in my room except the furniture."

"You can bring that too, if you want," I said. "We'll find a spot for it."

She shifted from one foot to another. "There's a desk. The front folds down. It belonged to my great-great grandmother. I think it's called a secretary? I'd like to keep it if I can."

"Clean anything out of it and Rebel will put it in the truck for you."

"I'll grab some boxes," Rebel said. He'd had the foresight to grab some this morning before coming over. We'd all ridden here in the truck, which meant everything she took needed to fit into the bed of the vehicle.

I took Madison's hand and went with her to the bedroom. I needed to see exactly what we'd be packing. If we needed a second truck, better to find out now. I could ask someone to bring one over. Hell. I hadn't even spoken to Atilla. He had no clue I'd told Madison to move in with me. Of course, I also hadn't cleared things up with her either. She didn't realize I planned for her to sleep in my bed. Even if all I got to do was lie next to her, it would be enough for now.

I scanned Madison's room, noting the bookshelf with well-worn paperbacks. Looked like my woman enjoyed reading. I'd have to take her shopping for some new books later. Aside from those, she had clothes, three pairs of shoes, and a handful of knickknacks on her dresser. It wouldn't take much to pack everything and get it loaded. At least we wouldn't need a second truck. On the other hand, I felt bad for how little she owned. I couldn't imagine what her life must have been like living with an addict.

"Rebel is getting the boxes. Why don't you start in here with anything you don't want the rest of us to touch? I need to make a quick call." I kissed her temple and walked out, but not before I saw her cheeks turn pink and heard her soft gasp. I smiled, enjoying her reaction.

"Did we bring enough?" Rebel asked in the hallway, holding an armful of flat boxes and a roll of tape.

"I think we'll be okay. Set up a few boxes for her, then ask what she needs you to do. I'm going to call Atilla."

His eyes went wide. "Holy shit. You didn't talk to him about her moving in with you?"

I shrugged and kept going, not stopping until I'd reached the truck. I leaned against the side and called the Pres, wondering how much he was going to chew me out. Even he would agree Madison couldn't stay here. Didn't mean he'd like the thought of her living with me, though. I'd fucked up too many times.

"This better be important," he said when the call connected. "Like the reason you needed two of your brothers and a truck this morning. Or why someone saw a woman leaving your house."

Well, fucking hell. Someone already ratted me out. Bastards!

"'Morning, Pres."

"Seriously, Truth. What the hell is going on?" he asked.

I wished I had a beer right about now. This wouldn't be a fun conversation, and as much as I didn't want to have it out here in the open, I didn't want to risk Madison finding out either. The last thing she needed was the stress over worrying if she really did have a place to stay.

"Remember me asking you about Madison yesterday?"

"Boy, I'm not that fucking old yet. My memory works just fine."

"Sorry, Pres. Look, Knuckles gave me a call last night. He knew Madison piqued my interest, and he thought she might be in trouble. So I went to check things out. Found her drugged and about to be traded. Her brother wanted to use her to knock down the debt he owed to someone rather questionable. But it's what the guy said that set me on edge. He swore *his* men wouldn't accept her as payment going forward. Meaning, the shithead brother probably owes multiple people money. She's not safe in her own home, Pres."

Atilla sighed. "Goddamnit, Truth. I can't very well tell you no. Not without being an asshole. The club isn't going to like this. Not after everything you've said and done since…"

"Since Jane," I said. "I'm aware. Can you let the club know she'll be living with me, and that she's deaf?"

"I'll call Church. Clearly you, Knuckles, and Rebel will be exempt this time. Give me an hour and everyone will be up to speed, and I'll knock some sense into anyone who decides to start shit over you having a woman. I'm assuming you're claiming her."

I smiled. "Yeah. She doesn't realize it, though. We only met yesterday. I need time. She's not the sort to just accept that she's mine. I told her she needs to pretend to be my girlfriend in order to stay safe, but I think I can win her over during that time."

"You fucking better. For now, I'll tell them she's staying with you. We'll talk about her being your old lady another time."

He hung up without another word and I went back inside to help Madison. By the time I got back to her bedroom, she'd already filled a box with clothes and struggled to tape it closed. I took the roll from her.

"Press the flaps down," I said. She followed my instructions, and I taped the box shut before loading her books into one of the smaller boxes. Pulling out my phone, I checked the hours for the local bookstore. It looked like we'd have sufficient time. Even though she'd have plenty of things to put away when we got home, I wanted to get her some new books to read.

It didn't take long to pack up everything she wanted to take. Rebel loaded most of it into the truck, then Madison did one last walk-through, saying goodbye to her childhood home. As much as I wished things had been different for her, I wondered if she'd have ever given a guy like me a chance if she hadn't needed my protection. Probably not.

Once we reached the compound, Rebel and Knuckles helped us unload. I hadn't thought to ask Atilla if I could hold onto the truck a little longer, but I didn't think he'd mind. I wanted Madison on the back of my bike, but I didn't think she would be ready for that just yet. Plus, I didn't want to limit how much she bought while we were out. I wondered if she knew how to drive. Was it even possible for her to, or would it be too dangerous if she couldn't hear things like a car horn or a siren? I'd have to ask her or look into the requirements. Either way, I'd need a vehicle other than my bike. One I'd fit into, and not some tiny-ass car.

Then again, if she could drive, I'd want something she felt comfortable in. Would she be okay with an SUV or truck? First I'd talk to her about it, then I'd research some vehicles. It wasn't like we were rushing out to buy something today. I had a feeling I'd have to fight her to accept something as expensive as a vehicle anyway.

Rebel placed the last box in my bedroom and waved as he walked out. Which left Knuckles. He and Madison were having a conversation in sign language, but both were speaking as they signed so I could follow along. I really did need to learn how to communicate with her. I'd never done well in school with foreign languages, but maybe this time would be different. Something involving my hands instead of my tongue might be easier for me.

"Madison, I'd like to take you somewhere. I know today had to be stressful for you, and I want to make it better," I said, facing her and letting Knuckles sign what I said.

"Where?" she asked.

"Bookstore."

Her eyes lit up and she clapped her hands together, then she immediately sobered. "But it's expensive."

"Then what if I give you a limit? Ten new books?"

Her mouth dropped open. "Ten? Do you know how much that costs?"

Not really. I read on occasion. Manga counted, right? No one in my club knew about my secret addiction. Then again, more than half probably didn't even know what it was. I doubted anyone else read Japanese comics or graphic novels. I had three apps on my phone dedicated to reading those stories. If I'd had any of the paperbacks in my house, my brothers would have given me shit about it. I figured if I dropped a hundred dollars a month on my reading habit, then there wasn't any reason I couldn't do the same for Madison.

"Then what if I said you could buy one hundred dollars worth of books?" She stared at me. Not saying a word. I wondered if I'd just broken her. "Is that too much?"

"Of course, it is!" She shouted the words, and I fought not to wince. I knew she could be sensitive about her volume when speaking.

"Well, we can discuss it more when we get there. I'm sure they have some on sale if you're worried about the cost. Do you ever read on your phone?"

Her cheeks turned pink. "I couldn't buy them. I don't have a credit card. When I bought our groceries or paid the utilities, I always used cash."

Right. Working part time at the bakery probably didn't line her pockets with extra cash. Not when she had to be responsible for so much at home. Things were going to change for her. Not only would I keep her safe, but she wouldn't have to worry about paying bills any longer. I wouldn't stop her from working, if it was something she enjoyed, but I wanted her to use that money for things she wanted and not what she needed. It was my job to handle all necessities. Of course, I still had to convince her of that.

"We can talk about it more later. Right now, do you want to shower and change? I think we're all sweaty from packing and moving your stuff."

Knuckles turned to me. "Even though I've been signing for you, I'm going to let the two of you go out on your own. You seemed to communicate just fine before I got here today."

"I need to learn how to sign."

He patted my shoulder. "Ask her to teach you. But I'm willing to help too. It's nice, seeing these changes in you. I think everyone will be pleased with this new side of Truth."

"Fuck off, asshole," I grumbled.

Knuckles told Madison bye, and then the two of us were left alone. I offered her the shower first, and then quickly washed up and changed. Before we left, I took a second to send a text to Atilla to let him know I'd need to hold onto the truck for another few days, then I drove Madison to the bookstore. I'd noticed the books on her shelf had price stickers from the thrift store on them, except for a few that she must have bought brand new.

The cool air felt great when we entered the store. Madison stared at everything, cheeks pink from her excitement. I followed behind as she checked out all the displays up front before wandering through each section. Since she didn't seem to like just one genre, I hoped she would pick a variety of books. No matter how many books she picked up, she always put them back down and didn't select anything.

"Nothing you want to read?" I asked.

"They're expensive," she said.

I picked up the last one she'd shown interest in, noting it was less than fifteen dollars. Handing it to her, I grabbed another title I remembered out of the ones she'd looked enthusiastic about.

"Now, that's a start. I want you to pick at least two more. If you aren't comfortable buying more than that, then we'll check out and leave. But I was dead serious when I gave you a hundred-dollar limit. Four books isn't going to bankrupt me, Madison. After everything you've been through, you need a way to escape reality for a bit."

Her brow furrowed, and I knew I'd said too much too fast, so I repeated it at a much slower pace so she could read my lips. She gave me a bashful smile and an awkward hug before selecting two more books. The woman was far too sweet for someone like me. Too bad. I never planned to let her go. Her asshole brother had given me the perfect opening. Now I had her in my home, and I'd show her how good I could be to her. I'd make sure she never wanted to leave.

After the bookstore, we stopped at the grocery store, where I had to battle with her again. The woman didn't like to spend my money and checked the price tag on every single item she touched. This wasn't going to be easy. Short of showing her the balance on my account, I didn't know how to make her understand I could afford to take care of her. At the same time, I worried if she knew exactly how much money I had, it might scare her off.

One day at a time. I'd call this a victory for now.

Tomorrow would most likely present an entirely different set of issues.

I smiled. No. Tonight would, when she realized

we were sleeping in the same bed. Anticipation hummed in my veins. I'd knock down her walls, one by one. Sure, I knew I was moving too fast for the average person. Nothing about our situation was remotely normal. I only needed her to see it that way too.

You're mine, little angel, whether you realize it yet or not.

* * *

Madison

He'd taken me to a bookstore, and insisted I get several new books to read. I still couldn't believe it. Even when my parents had been alive, they hadn't let me splurge like he had today. Then again, no one else in my family had loved reading as much as I did. The fact he'd asked if I read on an app made me wonder if he read frequently on his phone. If we read the same things, we could have discussions about our favorite titles and characters. I felt giddy at the prospect of having someone to talk to about my favorite subject.

Truth had put the groceries away while I unpacked. When he'd cleared out room in his closet and dresser for me, I'd hesitated. It didn't make sense for us to share a room in his house. He'd taken me in when I had nowhere else to go, had saved me at the risk of his own life, and I knew he was a good man. He'd proven it to me several times over in the short amount of time we'd known one another.

I eyed the bed. The same one I'd woken up in this morning, and I realized Truth slept on the opposite side. Had he been next to me last night and I hadn't realized it? Were we supposed to share the bed tonight? I didn't know what he expected from me. Not once had he mentioned sex.

You can sit here and worry about it, or go ask him. Right. No point in giving myself an ulcer over something that might not even be an issue. I could be inventing problems where there weren't any.

I called out his name so he'd know I was looking for him and searched each room. The last thing I'd expected was to find him in the second bedroom putting a bookshelf together. Cleo sat nearby, watching his every move. It surprised me that she wasn't trying to play with the loose screws or tools.

Two bookshelves already sat against the walls. He had three more huge boxes he hadn't even opened, and according to the writing or pictures on them, two contained chairs and the third had a small table. What was he doing?

"What's all this?" I asked.

"I'm making a library for you. Your books can go on the shelves, and you can sit in here to read whenever you want some alone time." He held my gaze. "If you're wondering why I didn't order bedroom furniture instead, we'll discuss it later. But I want you to know I will never hurt you, and I won't take anything you don't offer, so please don't think I'm going to force myself on you or something."

I held up a hand. "Speak slower. You sometimes go so fast it's hard for me to catch everything when I read your lips."

His gaze shot to my ear and he nodded, realizing I didn't have my hearing aid in. The battery had been low since I hadn't turned it off last night. I'd been amazed it lasted as long as it did. One of these days, I'd get the one I really needed, but it was roughly two thousand dollars, and I certainly couldn't afford it. Insurance refused to cover the cost, which was why I had some that were only a fourth of the price.

"I can't wear my hearing aid again until tomorrow," I said.

"Can you hear anything at all without it?" he asked.

I shook my head. "Even with it, I can barely hear out of that ear. I'm completely deaf in the other one. Am I yelling right now?"

He smirked and nodded. My cheeks warmed, but he hadn't said anything until I'd asked, so it clearly didn't bother him. I couldn't ever remember feeling so comfortable around someone before. Especially a stranger. Even my parents had made me feel self-conscious about my hearing loss. Although, could you call it a loss if you'd never had it to begin with? I'd been born deaf.

I sat on the floor, crossed my legs, and leaned back against the wall. Even if we couldn't talk right now, I could at least watch him work. Cleo ambled over and plopped down next to me. I petted her soft fur while we waited for Truth to finish. It only took him a moment to get back to putting the bookshelf together. Once he'd assembled it, he placed it alongside the other two. Even though he'd centered them on the wall, I could tell there would be space for at least one more. Not that I needed all those shelves with my meager collection. Why had he gone to so much trouble for someone only living with him temporarily? His thoughtfulness warmed my heart.

It didn't take much to put the chairs together, and he only had to screw the legs into the table. He placed it between the chairs in the center of the room. Truth folded his arms and stared at them before shifting them over to a wall. When he faced me again, he started speaking once he had my attention.

"I'll get a lamp for the table. Or maybe a floor

lamp."

"Thank you. I love it." I didn't get a chance to stand up before he'd left and returned with my box of books, as well as my sack of new ones. I eagerly placed them on the shelves. "It's perfect."

Truth placed his hands on my hips and tugged me back against his chest. I tipped my head to look up at him and saw him staring at my books. The look on his face seemed... I couldn't quite put it into words. But something told me he was pleased with the way the room turned out. Or perhaps it was more that he liked having my things here? I might not be experienced when it came to men, but even I could feel there was something between us. It had been an instant spark of attraction, and the more time I spent with him, the more I wanted to stay by his side. I wanted to know everything about him.

He stepped back and took my hand, leading me to the kitchen. A pad and pen sat in the middle of the table. He grabbed both and quickly wrote something, then showed it to me.

It's still too early for dinner, but do you want to eat here or go out? I'm fine with either.

He'd already spent so much on me today! I hated to ask for more, but was it really any better asking him to cook? I could do it. Would he even let me? I'd discovered most people equated my deafness to be completely helpless, or stupid.

"I can cook dinner for us," I said.

He reached over to cup my cheek before writing again. *I'd rather you rest tonight. You've had a long day with a lot of changes. Why don't I order something? Pizza? Chinese?*

I'd never had Chinese food before. I wouldn't even know what to order. And pizza... It reminded me of

Justin. When our parents first died, he ordered a pizza nearly every night for dinner, since he couldn't cook. Truth seemed to sense my hesitation with either option. He started writing again.

Or I could get someone to run out and grab some burgers for us. They won't mind.

"Are you sure?" I asked.

What do you want to order? Ever been to Big Bob's?

I hadn't, but I'd heard they were really good. I wrote down an order for a cheeseburger, fries, and soda. I didn't know if I could eat it all. My stomach had shrunk due to the lack of food at the house. My check only went so far.

Truth texted someone from his phone, then sat down at the table. He pushed out the chair beside him and I took a seat.

Is this easier than trying to read my lips? I read his message and nodded.

Can you teach me to sign?

Wow. Mrs. Johnson had learned a little. My brother had learned it along with my parents when I was just a baby. Except for them, no one had bothered to even try. It wasn't like they could use sign language as often as Spanish. To me, it was not only a useful skill, but a required one. To everyone else, not so much.

"I'd love to teach you." I signed as I spoke.

We spent the next half hour going over some basic words and phrases. By the time our food arrived, he'd picked up enough that I thought he might be fluent within a month. I didn't even make it all the way through dinner before I started yawning. It looked like Truth had been right about me having a long day. I'd woken up in a strange place, discovered my brother betrayed me in one of the worst ways, and had my life turned upside down.

By all rights, I should be freaking out. Instead, I felt oddly calm. For most people, a big guy like Truth would be scary. Instead of intimidating, I found his size to be comforting. When he'd put his arms around me earlier, I'd known no one would hurt me. Not as long as he stood by my side.

"Ready for bed?" he asked, signing the word *bed*.

"Yes. I'm sorry. I didn't realize I was so tired."

He put our dishes in the sink, rinsed them, then came to take my hand. He led me to the bedroom.

"You change. I'll make sure the doors are locked."

He left, shutting the bedroom door behind him, and I quickly changed into my pajamas. I'd already brushed my teeth and washed my face by the time Truth returned. He grabbed a pair of basketball shorts from the dresser and went into the bathroom. While I waited for him, I got into bed on the same side I'd woken up on this morning. My heart pounded in my chest. I still didn't know if we'd slept beside each other last night. Even if he we had, this was my first time knowingly sleeping next to a man. I found it both nerve-racking and thrilling.

Truth came out, turning off the bathroom light, then the bedroom light. He got into bed and reached over, lacing our hands together. I watched as he closed his eyes and took a deep breath before releasing it. Within a few minutes, I felt the vibrations of snoring and realized he'd fallen asleep already.

Any tension I'd felt up to that point, immediately went away. I turned onto my side, still holding his hand. A little moonlight filtered through the blinds, bathing his face in the silvery light. When we'd first met, his beard had been so wild I couldn't read his lips. He'd not only trimmed it, but it looked like he'd gotten a haircut too. Had all that been for me?

You treat me like I'm normal. No one's done that before.

I watched him for another few minutes before closing my eyes and going to sleep.

Chapter Five

Truth

The moment she fell asleep, I opened my eyes. I couldn't believe she'd thought I was actually asleep. Communicating with Madison wasn't easy. Of course, all the good things in life were usually hard to obtain, or you had to fight for them. I'd go to hell and back for the woman lying beside me. When Lynx said he'd known Meredith was it for him within minutes of meeting her, I'd thought he was fucking crazy. Same for Atilla and Maui. Then I'd met Madison. Now I understood all too well.

She took my breath away. It wasn't her looks, although I found her to be quite pretty. No, it was her spirit, and her sweetness. Despite everything dumped on her, she still found a reason to smile every day. She'd been kind to me, even when I'd yelled at her in the bakery.

Most women would have woken up screaming or losing their shit over being in a stranger's house. Not her. She'd taken it all in stride. Although, I had to wonder how much of that had to do with living with an addict all these years. How much had he put her through for her to be able to just roll with the punches? Cleo jumped onto the bed and curled up by our feet. She'd already accepted Madison as part of our family. The fact my two girls got along made me smile. No matter how much I wanted Madison to be mine, if she'd hated Cleo, I wasn't sure what I'd have done. There was no way I'd throw out my sweet cat.

"You're an incredible woman, Madison. I hope you know that. If you don't, I'll make sure you realize it. Whatever it takes, I want you to feel pride in who you are, because I've never met anyone like you before."

I knew she couldn't hear me, and since she was asleep, she wasn't reading my lips. Still, I felt better saying those words. One day, I'd tell them to her while she was awake. No, I'd sign them to her. She needed to see how invested I was in making this work between us. She might think I was only helping her right now, but it was more than that. Telling her was one thing. I wanted to *show* her. Something told me no one had ever done that before.

* * *

A fist pounding on my front door woke me. I eased out from under Madison, who'd curled into me during the night. As much as I'd have preferred to cuddle with her more, it was probably best for her not to discover how much she'd shifted in her sleep. Even if I hadn't been the one to drag her against me, it still might have freaked her out to wake up like that.

I shut the bedroom door and went to see who the hell was so impatient first thing in the morning. The Pres smirked at me when I yanked the door open, and I had a feeling I'd need to down a pot of coffee while listening to whatever he had to say.

"Isn't it a little early for a visit?" I asked.

"If it makes a difference, I have a Prospect bringing over some donuts. All you have to do is brew the coffee."

"Does Solena know you're eating donuts over here?" His silence told me enough. If she found out, he'd get in trouble for one of two things. Either for eating donuts without her and the kids, or because donuts were bad for him. "Just make sure she knows it wasn't my idea."

I started a pot of coffee in the kitchen and sat at the table while it brewed. The fact the Pres had come over so early didn't bode well. He already knew about Madison being here. Had Church gone so poorly yesterday that he'd decided she couldn't stay with me?

"How pissed is everyone?" I asked.

"They weren't happy, but I wouldn't exactly use that word to describe them either. However, if Madison weren't in danger, they'd have voted for you not to have a woman at your place. I spoke with Knuckles and Rebel this morning. They're going to talk to a few of our brothers and tell them what they've witnessed with you and Madison."

"Meaning the way I act like an idiot around her?" I asked.

He smiled. "Something like that. Knuckles said he'd noticed a big change just in the last twenty-four hours. Hell, he said the moment you spoke to her at the bakery something seemed different. Sometimes you just know when you've found your one and only."

"I haven't told her. She thinks she has to pretend to be my girlfriend in order to stay out of her brother's hands. Not my finest moment, but I thought if I outright claimed her, she'd take off running. This way I have time to win her over."

The coffeepot stopped percolating, so I got up to pour us each a cup. I knew Atilla took his black like I did, so I placed the full cups on the table and sat down again. In the past, I wouldn't have batted an eye at deceiving a woman. With Madison, it made me feel awful. Didn't matter if this was the only way to keep her safe right now and give me the chance to make her mine completely. She deserved my honesty. I only hoped it didn't come back to bite me in the ass later.

"The two of you need anything?" he asked.

"I picked up some groceries last night and took her to the bookstore. It's really fucking hard to get her to spend any of my money. She fights me every step of the way. After seeing her house and how very little she owns, I can understand. A few new books were an extravagance she couldn't afford. To me, it was nothing."

Atilla nodded. "I think Meredith likes to read too. So do Casey and Solena. Maybe the ladies could get together and discuss books at some point. Might be a good way for them to bond."

"Well, I did make a library for Madison last night. It only has two chairs, though."

Atilla choked on his swallow of coffee. He gasped and wheezed until he'd caught his breath. "Excuse the fuck out of me? What the hell did you just say?"

"I made her a library?" I asked, wondering what seemed so odd about it.

"Show me."

I shrugged, took another swallow of coffee, then stood and led the way to the spare room. It had already been empty, so filling it with some shelves and other furniture wasn't a big deal. I still needed to order a lamp for the room. No reason I couldn't get her two more chairs and another small table. It would be a good place for her to host a book club, or something similar.

Atilla let out a low whistle. "Still a bit bare, but I'm impressed."

"I'll get more shelves after we increase her collection. I thought three was a good start. You see how little she has, even with the ones we purchased yesterday. And yes, I'm trying to bribe her with a damn library."

"I bet she'd like some nice curtains in here," he said. "Maybe a picture or two. Although, I'd imagine you're trying to save the wall space for future bookshelves."

"I am, but there's no reason she couldn't hang something between the windows. I'm going to order a lamp today so she won't have to use the overhead light in here at night."

"What else do you have planned?" he asked, heading back to the kitchen and his cup of coffee.

Before I even had a chance to sit down, someone else knocked on the door. I hoped it was the donuts, since my stomach was now growling. Lucas was outside the front door and didn't say a word. He just offered me a large box of donuts and rushed off. Since I didn't think he had an issue with me, I was going to assume he had other orders to follow this morning.

I carried the donuts to the kitchen and grabbed a chocolate glazed before Atilla could snatch it. He glowered as I bit into it, and I didn't feel the least bit remorseful. Fucker had pulled me out of bed before I was ready this morning.

"I asked her to teach me sign language. I learned a little last night. It also made me curious about her hearing aid. If the one she has now doesn't allow her to hear very well, there has to be a better one, right?"

"I'd say ask her, but if she thinks you're going to buy it for her, she may not tell you." Atilla finished off his donut and reached for another. "Do you have plans with her today?"

"Nothing concrete, but she only has today and tomorrow off work. After that, she goes back to working at the bakery in the mornings. I'll have to speak with the owner. I can drop Madison off and pick her back up, but I need to know she'll be safe while she's in the shop."

"I can ask Officer Benson to keep an eye on the place, at least for this first week. Maybe if people see police patrol the area each day, they'll leave her alone while she's there. Besides, you aren't one hundred percent certain anyone will come for her. She could be out of danger already."

"I'm not willing to risk it," I said.

"Understandable. I'll ask Solena and Casey to drop by the bakery her first day back. They can introduce themselves. Might be best for them to meet away from the compound."

"Why?" I asked.

"Meredith and Casey can both be very protective of this club. Solena is to some extent as well, but I think she'd be less likely to intimidate your woman. And I'm not saying my daughter or Meredith would do it on purpose. You know they can both be sweethearts."

"Fine. I'll spend today finding out more about what Madison likes and needs. Once the women meet her at the bakery, ask them to drop by the house sometime. Tell them Madison has a library and likes to read. That should light a fire under them."

He chuckled. "You're not wrong. Although once they see all those empty shelves, they may very well bring her any books they don't want to keep."

"I'm sure it would thrill her to have more new things to read. It won't offend her to receive books someone already read. More than half of hers came from the thrift store."

Atilla finished his coffee and stood. "Let me know if there's anything the two of you need, or if your brothers act like assholes. Otherwise, I'll give the two of you some space for a few days. We don't have anything urgent on the books right now, so you don't have to worry about rushing off to handle any jobs for at least the next week."

"Thanks, Pres. And sorry for bringing her here

without asking first. I didn't really have time to run it by anyone. She needed me."

"I'm not angry about it, and once I explained what happened, the other officers were fine too. It helped that Knuckles was the one who called you. It meant you already had permission from one of the club officers."

Another knock at the door had me wondering who the fuck else was going to drop by this morning. I walked Atilla out and stared at Knuckles, General, Maui, and Spade. If Atilla had stayed, I would have had every officer in the club at my house. What the hell?

Knuckles handed me a large gift bag with a balloon attached to it, right as Rebel came up behind him. Was the entire club going to show up? "We put together a welcome package for Madison."

"She's still asleep," I said as I reached out to accept the bag. "But I'll let her know this is from the club when she wakes up."

"There's one more gift," Rebel said, handing me a box wrapped in pink paper. "I know you ordered bookshelves and chairs last night. Took a gamble on what you might need for the room."

I eyed the package. "Is it a lamp?"

He nodded. "One of those floor ones that has button you push with your foot to turn it off and on. It's kind of plain, but she can replace it later if she finds one she likes better. There's also a gift card inside the bag."

"For what?" I asked.

"Whatever she might want for the room. A rug? Hell if I know." Rebel smiled. "Madison is a sweet woman. I just wanted her to feel at home and let her know she's welcome here."

"I appreciate it." I eyed each man, especially Maui and Spade. If anyone would give me shit about having a woman in my house, it would be those two. Neither man said anything negative. "I'd invite you inside, but like I said, she's still sleeping."

"It's fine. We all have shit to do anyway." Knuckles waved and was the first to leave with Rebel right behind him. Maui lingered until the others had gone.

"Casey knows about Madison. I'm sure she'll want to meet her, but I'll ask her to wait a day or two."

"Atilla was going to speak to the ladies, I think. He suggested Solena and Casey go to the bakery where Madison works and meet her there for the first time."

Maui nodded. "Sounds like a good idea, and it will keep their first interaction short. I'm happy for you, but I have to admit I'm skeptical too. You don't exactly have a good track record when it comes to women."

"I know. I'll have to prove that she's different from the others and show you I'm not the same man when I'm with her. I'm not expecting everyone to be happy about this. Not right away."

Maui left, and I shut the door. Since I knew Madison would want to eat when she woke up, I took the gifts to the kitchen and sat them in one of the chairs. While the gesture was nice, I hoped it didn't make her feel overwhelmed. If she'd been hesitant to accept some books from me, how would she feel about an entire bag of gifts from people she hadn't even met yet? As curious as I was about the contents, I didn't look inside it. The present wasn't for me. It was only right to let Madison open it.

I rinsed Atilla's coffee mug and placed it in the dishwasher before pouring another cup for myself.

While I waited for Madison to wake up, I opened up the Tapas app on my phone and opened the comic I'd started reading the other day. I paid for six episodes before Madison wandered into the kitchen. She squinted at my phone screen, and I realized I'd been caught.

"Yeah, I read comics and manga." I folded my arms. "Doesn't really fit my overall image, does it?"

She sat down and reached for my phone. After scrolling through part of the episode, she got up and rushed out of the room, only to return with her own phone clutched in her hand. She held it out to me.

"Can you download the app for me?"

Seriously? I'd known she liked to read, but this certainly surprised me. In a good way. "I'd be happy to."

"How does it work?" she asked.

I tapped my ear. "Did you put your hearing aid back in? Should I get the notebook?"

"I'm okay. It's charged again," she said. "Just speak slowly."

"You pick which comics you want to read. Click the ribbon at the top right to save it in your library, and you can typically read the first three episodes for free. But they have special events so sometimes you can read more than that without paying anything. They also have some that unlock a new free episode every three hours."

I hadn't been this excited to talk to someone about something in a while. And no one knew I liked reading comics and manga. Now Madison knew something about me that I'd kept secret from everyone else. Although, I should probably let her know before she said something in front of my brothers.

"No one knows I read these," I said. "My club

would give me shit for it."

"I won't tell," she promised.

I noticed she had the cheapest iPhone available, and it was several years old. How much of a fight would she put up if I tried to buy her a new one? This might be one of those times I should just do it and coax her into accepting the gift after it was paid for. Otherwise, she might refuse to take it. Stubborn-ass woman.

"What's your passcode and password? There are some other apps I can download for you."

She told me and I quickly unlocked her wallet. When she wasn't paying attention to me, I quickly added my card information to her phone, then bought enough ink for her to read on Tapas for quite a while. After I downloaded the other two apps I used, and added the coins and points for each, I removed my card so she wouldn't realize what I'd done. Shit. She'd get an email.

I didn't like the thought of invading her privacy, but I opened her email long enough to remove the Apple receipt emails. Once I'd finished, I handed the phone back to her, then took a few minutes showing her how each app worked.

"The bag and box on the chair beside you were delivered this morning. My club wanted to give you a welcome present." I nudged the box of donuts toward her. "And my club President brought these."

She grabbed a donut and stared at the packages. I could clearly see she wanted to refuse, and at the same time there was a look of yearning in her eyes.

"You'll hurt their feelings if you don't open them," I said. Then I flat-out lied. "I told them I'd text to let them know what you thought of the gifts."

She grabbed the bag and started pulling out items.

They'd included a Harley Davidson T-shirt, a package of hair ties, a few tinted lip balms, and gift cards that would allow her to not only decorate her library but also buy more books. By the time she'd opened the lamp as well, she seemed stunned. My club had given her a generous amount of gifts, and I could tell at least one of the ladies helped. Possibly both Solena and Casey.

"It's too much," she said.

"No, it's not. You need to stop. I don't know why you feel you don't deserve to have these things, but you're precious, Madison. You've done something no one else has ever been able to accomplish."

"What's that?" she asked.

I grinned. "You tamed the beast. I'm not exactly known as a nice guy around here. Knuckles told me yesterday he could already see changes in me, for the better I might add. He thought it was good for me to spend time with you."

"So… this is more of a tribute for conquering the monster at the center of the maze?"

I threw my head back and laughed, not having expected that answer from her. And yet, it was rather accurate. The more time I spent with her, the more I wanted to hold on and never let go. There wasn't another woman like her in all the world. If ever someone was perfect for me, it was Madison.

Chapter Six

Madison

Why had Truth's club given me so many things? I hadn't met anyone except Knuckles and Rebel. Was Truth really acting different from how he normally would? I didn't understand why it was such a big deal. I felt confused on the best of days, but right now I was reeling.

Truth set up the lamp in my new library and said something about ordering more furniture for the space. He acted like I was going to live here permanently. The idea both terrified me and excited me. I didn't know why he wanted me to stick around. Did he get that butterfly feeling around me like I did every time I thought of him? I didn't think that was the sort of thing I should ask a guy.

Being at the compound, or going out with Truth, I hadn't had to deal with my brother. As much as I loved Justin, I now felt afraid of him. I hadn't trusted him before now, however knowing he'd wanted to trade me to settle a debt made me want to throw up. How could someone do such a thing to another human being? It didn't make any sense to me.

From watching the news, I understood there were monsters in the world. Murderers and rapists, among other bad people. Not once had I ever thought any of it would touch my life. Even when I realized my brother was using drugs and drinking too much, I'd never considered I needed to fear for my life just because we were related. What would have happened to me if Truth hadn't come to save me? It was a thought that kept pounding inside my skull. He'd saved my life. Of that I had no doubt whatsoever.

He'd left me in the library reading and said he

needed to take a shower. It wasn't until he'd been gone fifteen minutes I realized I needed the phone charger from the bedroom. I wished I could hear well enough to tell if the water was still running. I pressed my hand to the bedroom door, debating whether I should go in. What if he was changing? Knocking wouldn't do me any good. If he forgot about my hearing loss and simply called out to me, I probably wouldn't hear anything.

Slowly, I turned the knob and opened the door. I quickly scanned the room and didn't see him. The bathroom door hadn't shut completely, and I tried really hard not to look. I made it all of two steps toward the bed when I found myself gazing in that direction. And froze.

Truth had his head tipped back, eyes closed, and his hand wrapped around his cock. Every stroke, he said something. I couldn't hear him, but I'd have sworn I read my name on his lips. My cheeks went hot, and I felt an odd fluttery sensation inside me. I'd never watched porn, and while I'd read romances with sex in them, seeing something like this in person was vastly different.

I inched closer to the bathroom, spellbound. His hand moved faster, and after a few more strokes, he came all over the tiled wall. I must have gasped or made a noise because his eyes snapped open and focused on me. Stumbling back a step, my heart slammed against my ribs, and I wondered if I should run… but would I run *to* Truth or away from him?

His cock twitched and started getting hard again. Truth shut off the water and opened the shower door. Stepping out onto the mat, he held my gaze as he dried off. As he came closer, I found myself rooted to the floor. I couldn't have moved if I'd wanted to. Part of me felt like prey, while some other side wanted to preen like a peacock. The heat in his eyes told me he had indeed said my name while he'd done... *that*. It made me feel powerful.

The big biker was handsome as sin, had a body that could rival a god's, and yet he wanted *me*. I don't know why. I'd assume he could have anyone he wanted. Women had to throw themselves at him. I knew I wanted to, and I'd not once been tempted to do such a thing in my entire life. What was it about him that made me feel this way? Why was he so different?

He didn't stop until we were nearly toe to toe. Truth reached out and took my hand, then placed it in the center of his chest. I felt the hard *thump* of his heartbeat. I stared up at him, feeling a bit breathless.

"This is what you do to me," he said slowly so I could read his lips. Then the words he signed had my eyes burning with unshed tears, and any resistance I'd maintained crumbled to dust. *You're amazing. I can't stop thinking about you. I've never wanted anyone the way I want you.*

I didn't know how or when he'd learned that. The fact he'd even bothered made me even more emotional. That was the moment I knew without a doubt I was going to fall for Truth. It wasn't going to be a gentle glide, but a hard crash because he completely turned my world upside down, tore down every belief I'd held about myself, and ripped away all the doubts that men would ever find me desirable.

"I'm not going to rush you. We can go as slow as you want. You're in control, Madison."

I let my hand slide down his abdomen. When my fingers brushed against his cock, I felt the vibration in my throat letting me know I'd moaned out loud and not just inside my head. This was my first time to touch a man intimately. His skin felt smoother than I'd anticipated. He'd trimmed the hair and while I didn't understand why, it did give me a rather nice view of my fingers wrapped around him.

He reached out and lightly touched my chin, forcing me to look up at him again. "I don't have a lot of control right now, Madison. If you aren't ready for what comes next, I need you to leave the room while I finish getting dressed."

"What happens next?" I asked.

His eyes darkened. "I'll kiss you. Strip you. And make you scream my name."

I didn't have to be experienced to know what he meant. My only concern was how we'd communicate during sex. I didn't want to have to focus on reading his lips. Stupid hearing aid! If I had the better one, I might be able to hear him well enough that I wouldn't even have to keep my eyes open when he spoke to me. I'd never know until I tried it.

"What if that's what I want?" I asked.

"Oh, sweetheart. You shouldn't have said that. I was holding back. Now you've unleashed the beast inside me."

I shivered and my nipples hardened at his words and the fierce look on his face. He looked ready to devour me, and I eagerly anticipated what it would feel like. Did I need to tell him this was my first time? Did he already know? Despite having an addict for a brother, I'd led a relatively sheltered life. At least where men were concerned.

His mouth crashed against mine, and he kissed me breathless. I clung to him, wrapping my hands around his biceps. Truth picked me up, banding one arm around the small of my back. I dangled in the air and felt him working my shorts down my legs. He'd completely bared the lower part of my body before he eased me down onto the bed. Truth made short work of removing my pajama shirt and his gaze burned a path across my skin. I felt the heat of it all the way to my soul.

His lips closed over one nipple and I arched into him, my fingers sliding into his hair. I held him to me, never wanting to let go. No number of romance novels could have prepared me for the sensations flooding me right now. It was so intense it almost felt like too much all at once. He moved to the other nipple, licking and sucking it until my toes curled. The rasp of his whiskers against my skin only heightened everything. I'd never felt anything like it before.

He worked his way down my body, kneeling beside the bed. He kissed my thighs as he spread them wide. As much as I wanted to slam them shut, I forced myself to hold still and see what he would do next, and how it would feel. The moment he spread the lips of my pussy open, I felt a wave of heat wash over me, and I knew my cheeks had to be bright red. A single flick of his tongue was enough to make my brain shut down. Every thought I had flew away, leaving me unable to do anything except feel and respond physically. It was like a primitive side of myself had been unleashed, one I'd never realized I had.

He sucked and licked my clit, and as the pleasure built, I found my hips seeming to move of their own volition. I pressed closer to his mouth, never wanting him to stop. The pressure inside me built and built, until it finally erupted, and I screamed out his name. He didn't even give me time to catch my breath before he was over me and sliding into me. My eyes went wide at the pinch of pain, and the slight burn as I stretched to accept him.

Since I was looking up at his face, I caught the words *so fucking perfect* on his lips. And then he was driving into me, chasing his own orgasm as I still came down from the euphoric feelings of my first climax. I felt the heat of his release inside me and thought my heart might explode when I realized it meant he hadn't used protection. Not once had we discussed our past experiences, or whether or not I was on the pill. Which I wasn't. There was a good chance we'd just created a baby.

"Truth, I... I'm not..." I swallowed hard, wondering if I should even say something right now. Would I ruin the mood? Would he get angry? No. This wasn't my fault, and he wasn't the type to blame me.

He pressed his forehead to mine before kissing me again. When he pulled out, he hurried to the bathroom and returned with a wet cloth. He cleaned me gently before lying beside me and pulling me into his arms. Whatever I wanted to say would have to wait. I couldn't read his lips like this, so talking wasn't possible.

Most women would probably be terrified or furious right now. I didn't know what I felt. All my emotions were all over the place. I felt happy, sad, scared, excited, and so much more. He'd made a library for me. Brought everything I owned from my house. Why did it feel like none of this was temporary like he'd made it seem yesterday morning? Had Truth just tried to get me pregnant on purpose?

I didn't know how I felt about it. There were plenty of deaf women who had children. I knew it was possible for a child of mine to have a safe and happy life, especially with a dad like Truth. The way he took care of me told me he'd be an amazing dad. But it didn't mean I'd been ready for that step right this second.

Wait. Step. He'd said something about... what comes next. Was this what he meant and not necessarily the sex itself?

Suddenly, I realized I didn't know as much about this man as I'd thought. I'd felt like I was getting to know him rather well, and now it seemed I'd taken a few steps back. He'd called himself an asshole. Said he wasn't a nice guy. I'd not listened, deciding I knew better. But did nice guys try to get a woman pregnant on purpose?

Only one way to find out.

"Truth, can I ask you something?" He drew back so I could see his face. "You didn't use protection. I'm not on birth control. Were you trying to get me pregnant?"

He gave me an unrepentant smile. "And if I was?"

My breath caught as I tried to process his words. "But why?"

"Because it means I get to keep you, and there's nothing I want more, Madison. I told those men at the bar you were mine... and realized that's exactly what I wanted. Not for one night. Not as a temporary ruse. I wanted you to completely belong to me for the rest of your life."

He was insane. There was no other explanation. And yet, for some reason, I was finding this crazy side of him charming too. Maybe he wasn't the one who was nuts. It might be me who wasn't acting rationally. Who the hell wanted a man to do something like that?

Apparently, me.

* * *

Truth

Well, that hadn't been in my plans. I couldn't say I

regretted it. In fact, knowing I'd been her first, and would be her only, felt pretty fucking amazing. All right, so I'd been a dick. I hadn't used a condom or talked to her beforehand to let her know I was clean, or ask if she wanted kids right now. Or ever.

I knew it would be more difficult for her to chase a toddler or small child around, since she didn't hear like most people. Didn't make it impossible. Besides, I'd be here to help her, and so would the rest of the club. She'd never be alone. Even now, the brothers took turns watching the kids. Well, except me. Only Casey had trusted me with her daughter, Becca. I'd said some shit I shouldn't have, and pissed off Maui, but in the end Casey decided to give me a chance. I'd never understood why. Meredith and Lynx weren't happy with me, and even Atilla had glared at me when I'd gone near his children. Things would change now. My brothers could see I was becoming someone different.

"Can I ask you something?" She nodded. "Your hearing aid… you said you can't hear completely with it. Is there one that would give you that ability, or at least work better than the one you have now?"

"Yes, but they're really expensive. Around two thousand dollars. Some even cost more."

"I'm not worried about the cost, Madison. It kills me that you miss out on things because you don't have the equipment you need. If you'd lost the ability to walk, you'd need a wheelchair, right? Or if you didn't see very well, you'd need glasses. Your hearing aid isn't any different. It's something required to help you live an easier life."

She pressed her fingers to my lips. "Slower. When you get excited or passionate about something, you talk too fast for me to follow along."

"This is what I mean. If you had a better hearing

aid, that wouldn't happen as often, right?"

She shrugged. "I've never used one, so I don't know."

I'd find out what kind she needed, and I'd get her one. In the event that she needed a prescription, I'd go with her to the doctor and request the best hearing aid available. If I didn't have enough cash on hand, I'd hit up Atilla for some extra jobs until I had enough to cover it. I knew he wouldn't have a problem with me requesting it if he knew the money was to help Madison.

"Sorry I skipped the part of us discussing things in more depth before I took our relationship to the next level. I can only imagine how it made you feel."

"I was a little anxious at first and didn't understand why you'd done it. Hearing you say you'd wanted to keep me forever changed things. I didn't think anyone would ever want a life with me."

"For the record, I get tested regularly, and I'm clean. Haven't been with a woman since my last test, and you're now my one and only. I'll never cheat on you. I'd sooner rip off my nuts and bleed out."

She winced. "I could do without the visual, thank you."

"I didn't want you to think I did something like that without putting any thought into it. In fact, since the night I brought you home, I've thought of little else. Even before Knuckles called and said you needed help, I'd been making plans for meeting you again and asking you out."

"What happens now?" she asked.

"Well, I need to let Atilla know you're officially mine. I'm supposed to ask permission from the club and let everyone vote. He knows you're here, but officially making you mine is different. Since the club hasn't met you yet, and there's already a chance you could be pregnant, I'm going to request we skip that step. You'll get a property cut. It will be a smaller version of mine but will say *Property of Truth*. And before you ask -- no, I don't think I own you. It's just how things are done around here."

"So I'm officially your girlfriend? For real this time?" she asked.

"Think of it more like you being my wife. Other bikers will refer to you as my old lady. Doesn't have anything to do with your actual age. Which is…"

"Twenty-three. Isn't it a little late to ask?"

"Very true. In case you're wondering, I'm thirty-seven."

Her jaw dropped. "You're lying! There's no way. Maybe thirty, but thirty-seven?"

"Are you saying I've aged well?" I laughed softly. She was good for my ego. Not that it needed any stroking, but if she wanted to stroke something else… Nope. I wasn't going to go there. I knew she had to be sore. I might be an ass, but it didn't mean I'd treat her poorly. Perhaps I could have been gentler for her first time. Only Madison could make me lose control the way I had.

"We have the entire day to ourselves," I said. "Although, we've already used over half of it. Is there anything you'd like to do? Go out to dinner? A store you'd like to visit?"

"You don't have to take me somewhere all the time. If you turn the closed captions on, I can watch TV with you. While I can't hear the show, I can read along with it."

I gave her a slow smile. "Or we could watch some anime and turn on the English subtitles. There's a few in the original Japanese I've been dying to see. Want to give it a try?"

"It's something I haven't done before," she said. "But sure, I'll watch it with you."

She followed me to the living room, and after scrolling through the options under my various subscriptions, we finally selected something. It took less than one full episode before Madison was hooked. We binge-watched five episodes before we took a break. I wasn't sure how often she watched TV and worried it would strain her eyes or give her a headache, trying to constantly read the screen. Even if it did bother her, she'd never complain. I'd already learned that much about her.

I'd never spent so much time with someone. With Jane, I'd taken her out on dates, and we'd often gone to her place after dinner. Not once had she come to my house, and I'd never considered letting her move in with me. Madison wasn't a guest. It wasn't like I needed to entertain her. I didn't have an obligation to stay glued to her side, but until she knew the club better and had met the other ladies, I didn't feel comfortable leaving her alone in the house.

Since her brother was an alcoholic as well as a drug addict, I didn't want to drink a beer in front of her. What if it brought up bad memories? Or scared her into thinking I might become just like Justin? I'd talk to her about it at some point.

"Did you ever come up with a list of things you'd like to do when you had a boyfriend?" I asked. Her cheeks flushed and she looked away. All right. So she did have a list, but for some reason it embarrassed her. Now I really wanted to know what was on it. "You can tell me anything, Madison."

"There are a few things," she admitted.

I went to get the notebook and a pen, then handed

them to her. "Write down your list. We'll pick one thing to do today and save the rest for another time. Keep the list handy and you can add to it whenever you want."

"What if some of the things are expensive?" she asked.

"Don't worry about cost. Like I said, some we may not be able to do right now. Doesn't mean we won't ever check those off the list." I ran my finger down her cheek. "Think long term, Madison. I told you. This is forever for me."

She sat down with the notebook in her lap and stared at the blank page. Lifting her face to mine, she remained quiet for a moment before finally voicing the question I saw in her eyes. "It doesn't bother you? The fact we struggle to communicate?"

I kneeled in front of her. "Honey, does it seem like we can't talk to one another? It might not be perfect, but guess what? Two individuals without any hearing issues can still have trouble. Being able to hear what someone says, doesn't mean there won't be a miscommunication. I'm going to keep learning to sign, and we'll get you a better hearing aid."

"I'm not too much trouble?" she asked.

"Of course not. Why would you ever think that? Do you think I'm perfect? I'm not. There isn't a damn person at this compound who is." I paused. "Well, maybe Casey's daughter Becca. That little angel is as close to perfect as any of us will ever be. Until she becomes a teenager. Then all bets are off."

Madison shook her head. Humor flashed in her eyes, and I wondered what she'd been like as a teenager. Deaf kids were still exactly that… children. If anything, I'd think it would have made high school even more frustrating for her. Since she'd said her parents left the house to her brother, I wondered if they'd passed while she was still a minor. She hadn't brought it up, and I didn't want to open a wound that might not have yet healed. Life had a tendency to pile shit on people layer after layer. All of us struggled to fight our way through. Then there were people like Madison who had to do the same thing, except with fewer tools.

"Make the list, honey. Then we'll pick something together. We can call it our first official date."

She lit up, smiling widely, before she started writing. I left the room, but paused outside the door when I heard her talking to herself.

"A date. My first date ever!"

Shit. I hadn't even considered that. It had been clear she didn't have experience with men, but it never occurred to me she'd never had a boyfriend in her entire life. What the fuck was wrong with the guys in this town? Had they really let something like being deaf scare them off? Idiots. Their loss was certainly my gain.

While I gave her time to create her wish list of dates, I called Atilla. He needed to know Madison wasn't going anywhere. We'd only talked over coffee this morning. How had so much changed in less than a day? With Madison, things seemed to be going at warp speed. Instead of being scared shitless, I couldn't wait to see what tomorrow would bring.

The phone rang a few times before Atilla answered.

"Now what?" he asked when the call connected.

"Hello to you too, Pres."

"Seriously, Truth. What the fuck do you want? Didn't we use up our quota of bonding time this morning?"

I couldn't hold back my laughter. "All right. I get your point. I needed to tell you Madison is mine. Officially. I'm not asking. Not taking it to a vote. You said we'd discuss her stats later. Well, now's the time."

"Boy, better watch it. I'm still the President of this club. Last time I checked, none of your patches denote you as an officer."

"I wasn't trying to be disrespectful. I, uh... We slept together a little while ago. I didn't use protection, and she's not on anything, so..."

Atilla sighed. "You really are a dumbass. So you could have knocked her up already. Fine. I'll push it through. Make it seem like my idea. Can't have anyone thinking I've gone soft. You say this happened any other way than me telling you to claim her, and you and I are going to go a few rounds. And I don't mean verbal ones. This wasn't what I had in mind when I said we'd talk about it later. I'd planned to make you work for it a bit more."

"Got it, Pres. And thanks. I really appreciate this." I didn't want to push my luck. At the same time, I wanted Madison to feel welcome here. She needed to understand we were a family. Instead of being alone, she'd not only gained my support, but she now had a lot of brothers, and some women to call sisters or friends. "I think it would be good to do something for Madison as a way to introduce her to everyone. Not a party. I'm worried it would be too much for her. Something more low-key like a picnic or barbeque?"

"I'll talk to Solena. I think it's best we let the women take the lead on that one, but I'll make sure she's aware of your concerns with a party. I agree anything with that many people crammed into the clubhouse might make things difficult for your girl. That's the last thing we want."

I ended the call and went to check on Madison. What sorts of dates had she looked forward to all these years? Had she dreamed of having a boyfriend like a lot of other girls and young women? Since I hadn't had a sister, I didn't know much about females. Well, I knew how to get them out of their clothes, but not much else. Probably shouldn't tell Madison that. Not unless I wanted her to kick me out of my own bed.

She hadn't budged from her spot and had filled over half the page. With her hair tucked behind her ear, and a look of intense concentration on her face, she was too fucking adorable.

I sat beside her and waited until I had her attention before I spoke. "Did you pick something for today?"

She pointed to three different options. Getting ice cream at Sundae Breeze. Holding hands and walking in the park. Attending a festival. The first two were easy enough. As for a festival, I couldn't think of one going on right now. Did she know something I didn't?

"Festival?" I asked.

"There's a summer festival starting tomorrow in Parker Creek," she said. "We can't do that one today, but I've always wanted to go."

"Then we'll do that tomorrow. It's your last day before going back to work." I wanted to tell her she didn't have to go to the bakery anymore. Something told me it would be a bad idea. As independent as she was, it would blow up in my face. "Want to get some ice cream? We can always walk in the park afterward."

"We can really do both today?" she asked.

"Of course, we can. Let's shower and get ready. While we're out, you can decide if you want to eat dinner at a restaurant or we can make something at home."

She jumped to her feet and dashed out of the room. I liked seeing her acting so cute and carefree. It seemed like she was adjusting well to her new home, and to me. Still, I wouldn't breathe easy until I knew her brother wouldn't be an issue, or the men he owed. I needed to look into it, but I'd wait until Madison went back to work.

Right now, I only wanted to create lots of good memories with her.

Chapter Seven

Madison

Walking around the park last night, we hadn't garnered much attention. Or rather, I hadn't. I'd noticed women had a tendency to watch Truth. He hadn't paid them any mind. At first, I'd thought he didn't even realize they were staring. Was it something he dealt with all the time?

Being at the festival in Parker Creek wasn't nearly the same. I'd watched no less than four mothers grab the hands of their children and move far from Truth when they saw us coming. My heart ached for him. How could people be so cruel? I didn't understand. Was it his size? The fact he was a biker? It bothered me, knowing people judged him without making an effort to get to know him, same as they did with me. What a pair we made.

I held tight to his hand as he led me past the different vendors. Before we'd entered the main area, he'd told me to squeeze his hand whenever I wanted to stop. After stopping at just three tables, it became apparent Truth would purchase anything I showed even a little bit of interest in, making me more hesitant to pay attention to anything. He might not be hurting for money, but it didn't mean I wanted him to buy everything I liked.

Truth stopped and tipped my chin up so I'd focus on him. "Are you hungry?"

I looked around and saw a food truck with tacos. Pointing it out to him, I gave his hand a slight tug. Truth grinned and followed me. I hated speaking in crowded places, since I couldn't tell how loud my voice was. When we reached the truck, I pointed to the items I wanted and let Truth place our order. He found us a picnic table under a pavilion.

He reached out and ran his finger down my nose. "I'm worried you'll burn."

I signed back, *I'm okay*. It was one of the phrases I'd taught him already.

We ate in silence, but I could tell Truth had something on his mind. He kept scanning the crowd and watching me from the corner of his eye. Did he worry the men after my brother might be lurking nearby? I doubted they were the type to attend a town festival. I felt the table shake and looked sharply to the seats across from us. Knuckles smiled and gave me a little wave.

He slid a small package over me.

What's this? I signed.

From the club. Although, it was Truth's idea. Open it. Knuckles folded his arms and leaned them on the table, anticipation lighting up his face. What the heck had the crazy Savage Raptors done now?

I opened the bag and pulled out a box. When I realized what it was, my breath caught, and my heart skipped a beat. They hadn't. Had they? I looked at Truth, but he wasn't giving anything away. I opened the lid and saw one of the top-of-the-line hearing aids inside. One I'd never hoped to afford. How had they known exactly what I needed? I hadn't told them. But down to the very last detail, it was the hearing aid the doctor recommended.

It's already charged and ready for use. Knuckles pointed to it, clearly wanting me to try it out.

I removed the one in my ear and slipped in the new one. When I turned it on and adjusted the volume, tears sprang to my eyes. I could hear the crowd around us much clearer than before. While I'd been able to hear the overall noise, now I could pick up individual voices and bits of conversation.

I grabbed hold of Truth, staring up at him. "Say something. Anything."

His lips twitched like he fought not to smile. "Does it work?"

I nodded and couldn't hold back my tears. They slipped down my cheeks, and Truth wrapped me in his arms. I'd never been able to hear this well in my entire life, and I felt overwhelmed. Why had his club done such a thing? I hadn't even met most of them yet.

"Welcome to the family," Knuckles said. It was my first time hearing his voice so well, and I started crying again.

Truth leaned in closer, placing his lips near my ear. "Can you hear me?"

"Yes."

"You no longer have to struggle on your own, Madison. I will always take care of you, and any children we may have. You may have lost a brother, but you've gained many more. No arguments about the cost of the hearing aid. You needed it. This is only the beginning, honey."

I dried my tears and nodded. As much as I didn't like the thought of relying on other people, at the same time, it was nice to know I wouldn't be responsible for so many things anymore. It felt like I could finally breathe. Instead of fighting to survive every day, I could stop and enjoy myself, like today at the festival.

"A few of us are here. We'll stay out of your way since the two of you are on a date, but I wanted to get the hearing aid to you," Knuckles said. "If you need anything, give us a shout."

He stood and walked off. I saw him join three other men with the Savage Raptors cuts on. I didn't recognize them, so they were members I hadn't met yet. Truth had mentioned a picnic. He wanted me to meet everyone. While I could admit to being excited about it, the thought also scared me a little. What if they didn't like me?

"Finished?" Truth asked, motioning to my mostly empty food basket.

"Yeah. Can we look around some more?"

"Of course. I told you. Today is *your* day. We can do anything you want." He stood and threw our trash away before taking my hand once more. "Now you don't have to squeeze my hand to make me stop."

This was the closest I'd ever felt to being like everyone else. My hearing wasn't perfect in that ear, even with the expensive hearing aid. It was still the best I'd ever been able to hear anyone. I liked Truth's voice.

We wandered the festival for another hour. I selected two more small things and had some candied almonds. Truth stopped a few times and took a selfie with me, and always made sure to text a copy to me. They were our first pictures together, and I couldn't wait to take many more. On our way to the parking area, I froze mid-step. Near one of the booths stood a small child, crying so hard his shoulders shook. The expression on his face told me enough. A man stood in front of him, screaming, but the child only seemed confused and scared.

"Truth, I think something is wrong," I said, pointing to them. "Can we help?"

Truth led me over to the angry man and scared child. While he spoke to the adult, I kneeled in front of the boy. He had scarring that led me to believe he'd had a cochlear implant at some point. Was he deaf like me? The only reason to remove something like that would be if they would never work again. He might have lost all hearing now.

I signed as I spoke to him. "Are you all right?"

He took a shuddering breath, his eyes going wide as he nodded. When he signed and didn't speak, I knew he'd felt the same fears as me. He didn't want to talk in case people made fun of him.

My dad left.

Left? As in he'd gone somewhere and would be right back? Or had he abandoned his child?

"My name is Madison. What's yours?"

Liam.

I stood and faced Truth. "His name is Liam, and he said his father left."

He glared at the man. "Are you proud of yourself? You were screaming at a deaf child."

I didn't point out he'd apparently done the same to me when we'd first met, even if I hadn't realized it. The fact he was angry on the boy's behalf was enough. I felt small fingers close around mine and knew it was Liam. I held tight to his hand, hoping to give him whatever comfort I could. How long had he stood here, unable to communicate with anyone around him? My heart ached for him. I'd known that same pain many times in my life, and I'd never wish it on another person.

"What do we do?" I asked Truth.

"Did he say where his dad went?" Truth asked.

"No. He only said he was gone. You don't think he abandoned him here, do you? Could they just have gotten separated?" I scanned the area, but it didn't seem like anyone was frantically looking for their child. If my son got lost, I'd be losing my mind until I had him in my arms again.

Truth closed his eyes and tipped his head back. The tightness around his eyes, and the way he clenched his jaw, said it was likely the boy no longer had anyone. I knew we weren't going to walk off and leave little Liam here. Would the state be able to place him in a home where someone knew sign language? What if he didn't get the special care he needed?

"Can he come with us? Or should we find security and see if someone is searching for him?" I asked.

Truth looked at the little boy and kneeled down. He signed, *My name is Truth.*

I'm Liam.

More of the tension eased in the little boy and he pressed against my leg. I couldn't leave him here. It would kill me, walking away and never knowing if he was all right. How different would my life have been if someone had bothered to ask if I needed help, or not seen me as a hindrance? Part of me knew no one was looking for him. In my gut, something said this child had been left behind on purpose.

"Ask if he wants to go home with us," Truth said.

I signed the question and Liam nodded eagerly. It looked like he wasn't afraid, even though we were strangers. How could anyone leave such a sweet little boy? Was it the fact we could sign that made him so accepting of us? I hoped he wouldn't walk off with just anyone. What if a bad person got their hands on him?

"Come on. I'll call Wire on the way home. He's a hacker friend. Ask Liam if he knows his father's name, or what his last name is at the very least, and his age."

I quickly signed the questions Truth had asked.

My last name is Nance. I don't know my dad's name. I'm five.

I translated for Truth, and we followed him to the truck. Even though Liam was small enough he probably needed a car seat or something, I buckled him into the back seat and Truth drove carefully on the way home. He placed the call he'd mentioned, and it connected through the speakers in the vehicle.

I'd expected Wire to be a man, but a woman answered. Truth had said *he*, so maybe it was the man's wife?

"Wire is busy. Who is this?" the woman asked.

"What is it with no one giving a proper greeting when a call connects?" Truth asked.

"Truth?" she asked.

"Yeah, it's me, Lavender. I'd called to ask Wire for a favor, but it's something you could do just as easily."

She snorted. "If it requires my computer skills, I may very well do it better than him."

It amazed me I could hear the call as well as I did. I lightly touched my new hearing aid. It had to be the greatest gift I'd ever received.

"There was a deaf boy at the festival in Parker Creek, Oklahoma. He doesn't know his father's name and says he's five. Kid's name is Liam Nance. See what you can find? The boy said his father left him. We think he may have been abandoned."

"We?" Lavender asked. "Who else is there?"

Truth smiled. "My woman. Her name is Madison, and she's also deaf, but she can hear a little with the new hearing aid the club gave her."

"You've been busy," Lavender said. "Give me... I don't know. At least twenty minutes. Might take longer. I'll call or text if I find something. You didn't really give me a lot to go on."

"Thanks, Lavender."

The call ended and I reached over to take Truth's hand. I couldn't thank him enough for helping Liam. Was it wrong I felt torn over finding Liam's father? If the man really did abandon the little boy, I didn't want to give him back. He didn't deserve to have a kid as sweet as Liam.

At the house, I helped Liam inside and took him to the kitchen. I had no idea if he had food allergies, and when I asked, he didn't seem to know either. Deciding to play it safe, I stayed away from dairy and nuts when I made him a snack. I could hear Truth on the phone in the other room, as he paced back and forth, but couldn't make out what he was saying. He popped his head into the kitchen a few times to check on us as the minutes ticked by and turned into hours.

By dinner, I realized Liam was most likely staying the night with us. I didn't have anything for him to wear, or a place for him to sleep. Someone pounding on the front door startled me and I rushed to answer it when I realized Truth wouldn't.

A woman stood on the other side with a sleeping bag in her arms, as well as a large gift bag. "I'm Solena. You must be Madison."

I nodded. If she was here, it meant she was allowed inside the compound. Truth had mentioned there being a few other women. She must be one of them. Stepping back, I let her into the house, and she dropped everything in the living room.

"I brought the sleeping bag since I knew Truth didn't have another bedroom set up for the little boy, and even though I don't know his size, I brought a few things over for him to wear, as well as some toys." She blew out a breath, swiped her hair back from her face, and smiled at me. "I forgot to mention I'm married to Atilla."

"It's nice to meet you. Did they tell you Liam is completely deaf? He only knows sign language and hasn't spoken verbally."

"Truth told Atilla when he called. The clothes in the bag might not fit. You can exchange whatever is too big or too small. Unless you want to peek at his clothing size real quick? I could run take care of it now."

I stared at the bag, then the woman. "You went and bought him things?"

She shrugged. "Atilla's orders. No idea what's going on, but I was told he'd be staying here for now and would need the basics."

Leading the way to the kitchen, I introduced Liam to Solena, then asked what size clothes he wore. He didn't know but said I could check inside his shirt for a tag. Once I told Solena, she gave me a nod.

"That works. I bought a few things in that size. The ones that are bigger I can go exchange. At least he'll have some stuff for tonight and the morning. I don't want to overstay my welcome tonight, so I'll come by after breakfast."

Crap! Breakfast. I was supposed to return to the bakery tomorrow. I quickly texted Mrs. Johnson and told her I had an emergency come up and asked if I could have more time off. When she didn't respond right away, I had a bad feeling I was about to lose my job. Normally she answered within a minute or two.

Truth came back into the kitchen, looking more stressed than before.

"What's wrong?" I asked.

"Solena, Atilla wants you to go back home. I'm sure he'll tell you what's happening right now. I need to speak with Madison."

Solena hurried out the door, leaving me alone with Truth and Liam. I didn't know if the little boy could read lips, or could read at all. I showed him the sack with the clothes and toys, then left him in the living room to play for a little bit.

"Is everything okay?" I asked once Truth and I

were alone.

"We think Liam was actually bait," Truth said. "His father is Luca Nance. While there's no criminal record for the dad, the uncle is another matter. Luca has one brother. Angelo Nance. Their mother was Italian. Father was American."

"I'm confused," I said.

"Angelo works for one of the men running drugs in Bryson Corners. Your brother owes them a lot of money. While Lavender couldn't find anything concrete, she believes they used Liam as a way to lure you out. I think they wanted to snatch you and use you as leverage to get their hands on Justin. I'm betting they have eyes on the compound and followed you, hoping for an opportunity to grab you."

A chill went down my spine. Was someone watching me? Did they want to hurt me all because of my brother's stupid choices? But even worse, how could someone use a child as bait? "And Luca allowed this to happen to his son?"

Truth rubbed his eyes, and I could tell whatever he said next was something weighing on him. "The boy hasn't been treated well since his mother died six months ago. I'd imagine it was hard taking care of him, and the dad wanted a way out."

That poor little boy. What would happen to him now? And what the hell had Justin been thinking? How could he owe so many awful people money? I now knew there was no way to save my brother. I didn't see how anyone could get him out of this mess.

"What happens now?" I asked.

"Well, we have a few options. Let's figure out how to handle Liam's situation first. The woman I spoke to earlier is crazy talented. There's not much she can't do with a computer. Do you want to keep Liam?"

"You mean… adopt him?" I asked.

"Sort of."

I didn't know what that meant. "Yes, I want him to be our son. Are you okay with that?"

"More than." Truth smiled. "I'll let you tell Liam about it. Right now, I need to make some calls and I need to run an errand. Stay in the house with Liam, all right? You'll both be safe here."

He kissed my forehead, and it wasn't long before he left the house and I felt the rumble of his bike. Except this time, I could hear it too.

Chapter Eight

Truth

On my way to Officer Benson's house, I called Wire and Lavender back. When the call connected, I didn't even give them a chance to speak.

"Do it. She wants Liam to be our son. So whatever it takes, make sure no one can take him away from Madison."

"Weren't you the one complaining about my phone etiquette earlier?" Lavender asked.

"I'm running out of time. Have a cop to speak with, and I want to make sure that boy is safe. I also need you to forward me everything you've found so far on Justin and the men who want his head. If there's even a chance I can save Madison's brother, I'm going to do it. I personally want to bury the fucker, but he's her family."

"You should have everything now," Wire said. "And yes, you're on speaker. It's just the two of us home right now."

"Anything I need to know about Liam? I get the feeling you didn't tell me everything."

"Damnit, Lavender." I heard Wire harshly whispering to her, even though I didn't know what the hell he was saying. Clearly, she'd kept something from me. "Look, the kid hasn't had an easy life. From what we could find, he had cochlear implants until a year ago. He's now completely deaf, and nothing will ever make him hear again. The mom died in an accident six months ago. Since then, the father has left him with random people."

"When you say left him, you mean overnight or for a few days?" I asked.

"A mix of one night and as long as a week. He

doesn't seem concerned whether or not the people actually care for his kid. Did you have any trouble getting him to go with you?"

"No. But Madison used sign language to speak with him. I'd thought knowing they were similar had set him at ease."

"It could have. I'm sure all the chaos in his life helped him go with the flow," Wire said. "By tomorrow morning, the boy will be yours. So I don't have to go digging into your past, give me your actual name so I can put you and Madison on the papers. Do you know her last name?"

I heard more whispering. Then Lavender said something that nearly had me stomping on the brakes. "We only need your name. After all, it's best for a family to all share the same surname, right? So we'll just make Madison your wife while we're at it."

What the fuck? I knew they did this shit all the time, but it still took me a bit by surprise. I wasn't sure how Madison would feel about it. Then again, she might prefer a marriage over what I'd offered so far.

Shit. He wanted my name. I haven't even told Madison yet. The thought hadn't occurred to me until just now. How long had it been since anyone called me something other than Truth? Hell. I'd need to talk to Madison about more than Liam and her brother when I got home.

"My name is Xander Hundley," I said.

"All right. By morning, you'll have paperwork for Liam Hundley and Madison Hundley. Does your wife have a driver's license?"

"I haven't had a chance to talk to her about that yet. I'd considered buying her an SUV, but I'm not sure what requirements need to be met for a deaf person to drive."

"It differs from state to state," Wire said. "I'll check the guidelines for Oklahoma, and I'll include that in an email I'm sending you later tonight. If she already has a license on file, we can update her name and have a new one sent to your house."

"And if she doesn't, then you'll have all the papers you need in order for her to obtain one," Lavender said.

"Thanks. Now about Justin. I'm going to see if I can strike a deal with Officer Benson, or maybe he can get me in touch with someone who can. Either way, I want him out of Madison's life, but I know it would set her mind at ease if she knew he was safe somewhere."

"The files I've sent should help broker a deal with the DEA," Wire said. "They'll probably put him into protective custody. Considering the drug cartels involved the higher up the chain you go, he'll have to move and change his name when all this is over. As far as the smaller fish go, we'll handle it. Scare them. Do whatever is necessary to make sure they leave Madison alone. You have enough to deal with already. This is something small we can handle without having to even leave the comfort of our home."

"Thanks. I appreciate it. I'm pulling up to the house now. Let me know if anything else comes up," I said, then ended the call. I got out and walked up to the front door and rang the bell.

A sweet-looking woman answered, smiling up at me. If my cut bothered her, she didn't show it.

"May I help you?" she asked.

"I was hoping your husband was home. I'd like to discuss something with Officer Benson," I said. "Please tell him Truth with the Savage Raptors has some information for him related to the drug problem in Bryson Corners."

She nodded. "You want to come inside and wait?"

I followed her into the house and waited in the front entry. Looking around, I could tell they had kids. Did his wife always let strangers into their home? What if I'd been a bad man? I could have hurt her. Killed her. Taken their children. She seemed a little too trusting. Or maybe she was just that confident her husband would keep her safe.

Officer Benson came from the back of the house and gave me a hard look. I held up my hands. "I'm unarmed. I really do have information for you, but I need to give you some background first."

"My kids are out back. We can sit in the kitchen."

He pulled out a chair at their table and pointed to it. I sat and he took the spot across from me. I noticed he'd put himself between me and the back door.

"My wife has a brother named Justin. He's an addict, and he owes a lot of money to some big players in town. A friend compiled some papers for me, drawing the connection between the mess Justin is in, and some major cartels. Interested?" I asked.

"First, what do you want? I know this can't be free."

"My wife will worry about her brother. I want him out of her life. I thought maybe the DEA could offer him a deal, get him away from Madison in exchange for him testifying in what could be one of the biggest cases of this decade."

"All right. Second, why me? You could have called the precinct or gone to the DEA directly. Yet you're in my house."

"I've heard you're trustworthy. I know you're friends with Outlaw. So, do we have a deal?" I asked.

"I can't speak for the DEA but give me what you have and I'll see what I can do. I'll have to come up with some explanation as to how I obtained the information." Officer Benson ran his hand down his face. "Jesus. You didn't come with a small ask, did you?"

"Sorry about that."

He waved me off. Officer Benson pulled a business card from his wallet and slid it over to me. "Get the information to me at this email address. Find a way to send it anonymously. I mean, in a way even someone like Outlaw couldn't trace, you get me?"

I knew exactly what he meant. I took the card and then stood. Even though I didn't have anything concrete in place, I'd at least gotten the ball rolling. Now the issue with Justin was out of my hands. One less problem to deal with.

I didn't know what to expect when I got home. Walking into the house, I found Liam in his sleeping bag in the living room, and Madison curled up on the couch with a book. It looked like our new son had fallen asleep before dinner, and little Cleo had cuddled up beside him. Then again, Madison had given him some snacks. He may still be full. The poor kid had such a rough day. From what Wire said, Liam's life had been hard since his mom died.

"You're home," Madison said.

"Yeah. We need to talk. Are you hungry? We could make dinner together."

Her cheeks flushed. "Knuckles came by to check on us. I wasn't sure how long you'd be gone, so I asked him to order pizza. He said he'd get two in case you were hungry when you came home. It's due to arrive any minute."

"All right. I know us talking won't wake up Liam since he can't hear. Anything I should watch for?"

"Vibrations," she said. "He can feel your

motorcycle when you come and go. The door slamming. Things like that."

"I'll make sure to be careful in the future." I sat beside her and reached for her hand. I needed to tell her we were married and try to explain how. She'd need a ring. "Remember the woman I spoke to earlier? Lavender?"

"Yes. She seemed nice. You said she's good with computers, right?"

"Ever heard of hackers?" I asked.

"Who hasn't? They're popular in movies and books. Are you saying that's what she does?"

"Both her and her husband. I called them when I left here. By the morning, Liam will be our son, and you'll be my wife."

She tensed. "What? Wife? I don't understand."

"They're most likely going to hack into whatever government offices handle marriage licenses and such. When I was talking to them, I realized I never told you something important. My name." I laced our fingers together. "I go by Truth now, which is my road name. The name on my birth certificate is Xander Hundley. When it's just us at home, you can call me Xander. Only you get to call me that."

"What if I accidentally use that name when we're around other people?" she asked.

"It would be a problem, especially around my brothers or another club. Why?"

"Then it would be better for me to keep calling you Truth. It's not like I mind. It's the only name I've known until now. The fact you told me your real name is enough."

I didn't know what I'd done to deserve such an incredible woman. I knew I was a lucky bastard. Hell, every man in this club would say she was too good for me. They'd be right, but it didn't mean I'd ever let her go.

"Officer Benson is going to see what he can do to help Justin," I said. "But it's going to depend on your brother. Wire and Lavender found some information not only on the men your brother owes money to, but their bosses, and their bosses' bosses. This goes all the way up to some big cartels. It's like a wet dream for the DEA to possibly take those fuckers down."

"How is that going to help Justin?" she asked.

"If he agrees to testify, they might be willing to help him get clean, and give him a fresh start. It would mean you'll never see him again, and he'll have to move elsewhere. Possibly even out of the state."

"So I won't see him again, but he'll be alive and I'll be safe?"

"Right. At least, that's my hope. I have no idea how this will play. It may blow up in our faces, or Justin could refuse to cooperate. It's also possible the people after him could take him out before the DEA gets its hands on him."

She sighed and leaned her head against my shoulder. It was a lot for her to handle. While she may have lived with an addict, in many ways she'd lived an innocent life. Now that she was part of my world, things would be different. She couldn't wear rose-colored glasses and survive. If Madison thought she'd seen the darkness in the world already, she'd be wrong. All she'd done was play in the shadows a bit. I knew the horrors that were really out there, and I'd do anything to keep her safe. Even if it meant painting her some ugly pictures. Ignorance wasn't always bliss… it could get you killed.

"Once all this is over, things will settle down a bit. I can't promise it will remain peaceful. There's always something going on. Solena's son ended up with human traffickers. Meredith had a miscarriage. Now we're dealing with your brother's problems in order to keep you, and now Liam, safe."

She looked over at the boy sleeping soundly. "Our son. We're really a family, aren't we?"

"Yes, we are. The two of you are now the most important people to me. I will always have my club's back, but you're my top priority. Both of you."

"I'll be meeting everyone in the club soon, right? And so will Liam. I'm a little worried. Since he only knows how to communicate with sign language, it won't be easy for people to talk to him. Except Knuckles. Is there anyone else here who knows sign language?"

"I don't think so." Honestly, I'd never asked. Hell, until Knuckles started signing at the bakery that morning, I'd never known he could do that. Who knew what knowledge my brothers had? We each had things people didn't know about us. "Are you going in to work tomorrow?"

"No. I told Mrs. Johnson I had an emergency. She never responded, which makes me think I may not have a job anymore."

"Well, I wasn't going to bring it up, since you seemed to enjoy working, but things have changed now. There's no reason for you to have a job unless you want one. I have plenty of money to take care of us. We don't have to pay rent on the house. The utilities are paid by the club as well. Only thing I pay for, other than groceries and gas for my bike, are my movie channels and stuff like books, parts for the bike, and other non-essentials."

"How can the club afford to pay for everyone's electricity and water?" she asked.

"Before Atilla pays any of us, each month he takes the full amount of the utility bill, then divides it evenly among all of us. Well, not the Prospects. Only patched members."

"I feel like there's so much I don't know," she said.

"There's plenty of time. This is your home now, Madison. No one expects you jump right in and know everything about our club or how things work around here. There's a learning curve. At least you can hear well enough now that you'll be able to speak with everyone, and you seem less anxious than before."

She reached up and touched her hearing aid. Best investment I'd ever made. While everyone chipped in, I'd covered the bulk of the cost. Knowing she felt self-conscious about speaking in front of people, and struggled to have conversations without sign language, had bothered me.

Things would be different now. In so many ways.

I stood and held my hand out to her. Closing my fingers around hers, I helped her off the couch and led her to our bedroom. Since Liam was asleep, I hoped it meant we had a little time to ourselves. Once hadn't been enough, and this time, she'd be able to hear me.

Shutting the door, I twisted the lock and removed my cut. Madison's eyes went wide when she realized what was about to happen. She licked her lips and watched as I removed my boots and clothes. The heat in her gaze made my cock twitch in anticipation. I reached for her, and slowly undressed my beautiful woman, kissing every inch of skin from her collarbones to her knees.

"Truth, I... I need..."

I ran my fingers over her slit, and realized she was already wet and eager. As badly as I wanted to romance her, take my time worshipping her, I knew there was a little boy in the other room who could wake up at any moment.

"This is going to be quick," I said. "Liam could come looking for us."

"It's okay. I feel empty and need you inside me."

"Not yet. You're going to come at least once before then." I toppled her to the bed and spread her thighs. The second my tongue swiped across her clit, she gasped and arched into me. I traced circles around the hard little bud, then flicked across it twice before teasing her some more. Madison whimpered and I felt her body trembling. "Can you hear me?"

"Yes. Please, Truth. Don't stop."

"I'm going to make you come, then I'm going to flip you over and take you from behind." Since she was still new to this, I hadn't wanted to startle her. Best to let her know ahead of time what to expect, at least for now.

I went back to licking and sucking her clit until she writhed beneath me, begging me to let her come. Easing a finger inside her, I pumped it in and out while sucking on her harder. Madison cried out, her pussy clamping down on my finger. Before the orgasm had even faded, I had her face down over the side of the bed and slid in balls deep.

"You're so fucking tight. Wet. Complete perfection." I nipped her shoulder. "You're mine, Madison. No other cock will ever enter this sweet pussy. You'll only be filled with *my* cum. Tell me you want it."

"Yes! Yes, I want you to fill me up."

I growled and felt my balls draw up. I wasn't going to last much longer. "Tell me you want my baby."

"Please give me a baby. Truth, I'm so close. I

need... need..."

I felt her pussy clench, then the heat of her release. Unable to hold back another second, I fucked her so hard the bed started to scoot sideways. I let out a roar like some savage beast when I came, pumping my hips until I had nothing left to give.

Collapsing onto the bed, I dragged her into my arms. We'd need to clean up, but right now, I just wanted to catch my breath and hold her close.

"Will it always be like this?" she asked.

"No. Sometimes it will be better." I kissed her softly, thanking whoever had placed this woman in my path. I knew without the slightest doubt she'd been made for me. There was no one more perfect in all the world.

* * *

Madison

Liam missed dinner and slept until the sun came up this morning. To make up for it, I made him a big breakfast with eggs, bacon, and toast. As much as I'd have preferred to know for certain if he had a food allergy, I also didn't want to deny him yummy things if it wasn't necessary. I'd watch him carefully the next few days in case he had an allergic reaction to anything.

Liam, I have something to tell you. He kept chewing his food and stared at me, waiting for me to continue. I kept signing, hoping he wouldn't be upset by the news. *Truth and I have adopted you. You're going to live here with us from now on.*

He set his toast down and seemed to shut down before my very eyes. It was like a mask slid into place. I'd never seen a small child do such a thing before. What had the poor boy been through since his mother died? Then it hit me. When I'd said we'd adopted him, had he thought we were trying to replace his family?

You can still call us by our names, Liam. We aren't trying to take the place of your family, but this will be your home now. You'll be safe here, and we'll set up a bedroom for you. In fact, I bet Truth is already working on it.

Still nothing. I reached out and lightly ran my fingers through his hair. I wanted to hug him, to tell him I'd love him forever. Something told me it wouldn't be well received. He clearly missed his mother, and I couldn't blame him. All these years later, I still wished I could see my parents one more time.

Eat your breakfast. We can talk more later.

I started cleaning up the kitchen, trying to take the pressure off Liam. He didn't need me clinging to him or watching him eat. I'd thought we'd connected last night. He'd trusted me, came with me willingly. Why had he done that if he was going to put up walls today? Was it learning that we'd adopted him? I could imagine discovering something like that might be scary for a small boy.

Truth and I hadn't discussed this part. We'd thought he might be happy about the adoption. I should have known better. Even if Liam's father was a piece of shit who hadn't wanted him, he was *still* the little boy's dad. Small children were often like puppies. You could kick them, and they'd still want your affection. How could I reach Liam and make him understand? No, not just understand but accept the direction his life had taken.

Would the picnic interest him? Truth had asked the club to move it up to today since I wasn't going in to work. Actually, I'd never be going in again. When I still hadn't heard from Mrs. Johnson this morning, I'd told her it would be best if I put in my notice. *That* had gotten a reaction from her, and she'd accepted my resignation effective immediately. It made me wonder if she'd ever liked me working there. I'd thought she'd been nice. She'd offered me a job when no one else in town would. Why had she done it if she was so eager for me to leave?

I'd never understand people.

Knuckles came into the kitchen, startling me. If he'd knocked on the door, I hadn't heard him. Behind him, I saw three more members of the club walk past, each carrying furniture. It seemed Truth had called in reinforcements to get Liam's room ready.

The biker sat beside Liam and introduced himself.

Hi, Liam. My name is Knuckles.

The boy giggled. *That's a funny name.*

Yeah, I guess it is. Knuckles looked over and winked at me. Had he known I was going to have trouble with Liam this morning? I didn't know how, unless he'd been around a lot of small children and assumed Liam wouldn't react well to the adoption news. *What kind of things do you like to do? Do you have a favorite color? Mine is green.*

Cars and trains, Liam signed. *My mom bought me a big train set for Christmas one year. But my dad broke it after she died.*

I clenched my hands, wanting to rush over and wrap my arms around him. It took a lot to hold myself back. I filed away the information on the cars and trains. Maybe I could find out what kind of set his mother had bought him. If we got him the same one, we could tell him it was a way of keeping his mother with him. He might like that.

Knuckles continued to talk with Liam. While he occupied my new son, I went to check on Truth. He and the other three men were in the process of shifting the furniture and spreading a throw rug. When had they even brought one inside? I realized it wasn't a rug. Not exactly. It had roads, trees, and homes on it. Liam would be able to play on it with his cars. Solena had brought a handful last night, and I saw two more packages of them on the new dresser.

"Madison, this is Stinger, Ravager, and Maui. Guys, this is my wife, Madison."

I gave them a small wave. "It's nice to meet you. Thank you for the hearing aid, and for helping with Liam's room."

The one he called Ravager came over to shake my hand. "It's nice to meet you, Madison. I already had this furniture made, but no one had bought it yet. I was glad to be of help."

I studied the pieces again. "You made these?"

Ravager nodded. "It's something I enjoy doing."

"My wife is eager to meet you," Maui said. "She's home with our daughter right now. Becca is a bit of a handful."

"Will they be at the picnic?" I asked.

"You bet. The entire club will be there. Kids too. None of us thought Truth would ever settle down. He's not exactly known for trusting women. The opposite in fact," Maui said.

"Are you trying to start shit?" Truth asked.

"Only speaking the truth," Maui said.

"Give it a rest," Stinger said. "Atilla obviously approved of them being together. You really want to piss off your father-in-law?"

"Yeah, yeah. I'm more worried about Casey than Atilla," he muttered.

"Liam said he likes trains. His mother bought one for him as a Christmas present. Do you think there's a way to find out which one she'd bought? I thought we could get the same one, so he'd have something to keep her memory alive. I know it won't be the one his mom gave him, but if it's the same model maybe that would be enough. Do you think that will matter?" I asked.

"I'm not sure we could find out which train he had," Ravager said. "I'm assuming you can't get the original because something happened to it? But we could give him something better."

"Like what?" Truth asked.

"A train table with a built-in track. I've never made one before. It would be a challenge, and one I'd enjoy," Ravager said.

"If you're up for it, I think it would be great. It might be just what Liam needs right now," Truth said.

I backed out of the room, letting the men plan the train table and work on Liam's room. I'd wait and see it once they had it finished. Knuckles and Liam had moved to the living room, and the TV was on. I hadn't thought to ask Liam if he wanted to watch anything. I'd even forgotten to ask if he knew how to read. Most five-year-olds couldn't read well enough to follow along with closed captions. I was sure there were exceptions, though.

"What are the two of you watching?" I asked and signed.

Paw Patrol, Liam answered.

"Can he read?" I asked Knuckles. "I didn't put the TV on last night because I wasn't sure, and I worried asking him might upset him."

"A little. Mostly, he likes watching. Even without hearing or reading what's going on, he's able to follow along enough to enjoy it."

"All right. I'll make sure he gets TV time each day, then." I joined them on the couch. "I heard the picnic would be today."

Knuckles nodded. "In about another hour. Don't worry about bringing anything. Since the picnic is for you and Liam, everyone else is taking care of the food and drinks. Atilla had one of the Prospects go out and get some of those pop-up canopies. He wanted to make sure there'd be plenty of shade for the kids."

I'd finally meet everyone. Although, the more people who dropped by the house, the more it felt like I'd already said hi to everyone. Were there still more bikers to meet? I knew there were two other women, and I hadn't met any of the children. Would Liam enjoy playing with the kids?

Chapter Nine

Madison

I'd changed into a pair of shorts and a tank and put one of Liam's new outfits on him. Even Truth had changed before we left to meet everyone for the picnic. When Knuckles mentioned a few canopies, I'd thought of the small ones I'd seen the one time my parents had taken me to the lake. That wasn't close to what Knuckles meant. The giant canvas sunshades covered a large enough area everyone could sit under them comfortably, and the kids had space to play.

Along the edge of one area, they'd set up long tables and filled them with food and drinks. There were multiple folding tables and chairs, and I made my way over to the one where the women were sitting. Solena saw me and waved. I was glad I'd at least met her once. I felt a little more comfortable.

Solena stood when I got closer. "Madison, it's good to see you again. I wish we could have spoken a bit more last time."

"Hi, Solena."

"I'm Casey," the younger woman said with a bright smile.

"And I'm Meredith." The other woman stood and held out her hand. I gave it a quick shake. "Welcome to the Savage Raptors family."

"Thanks. My son, Liam, is like me. He can't hear. Except even a hearing aid won't help him. Right now, only Knuckles and I can speak with him. Truth is learning sign language, but he isn't proficient yet."

Solena patted my arm. "Don't worry about it. The kids will encourage him to play. I already told them he can't hear, so they won't be surprised."

"You should grab a plate of food," Casey said.

"Then come talk to us. It's nice to have another woman here. Not that I don't love spending time with Solena and Meredith."

"I did tell Atilla the other men needed to find women and settle down. It never occurred to me Truth would be one of the first ones to fall." Meredith shrugged. "Honestly, he's kind of an asshole to women. I didn't think anyone would want him."

I frowned and tried not to be offended by her words. And I failed. How could she say such a thing about the sweetest man I'd ever met? He'd been so gentle and kind to me. We'd been strangers when he'd rushed out to save me. Was this why he'd called himself an asshole? Did people actually say it to his face? He might be rough around the edges, but the man had a heart of gold as far as I was concerned.

"Do any of you know how I ended up living with Truth?" I asked.

Meredith and Casey shared a look before they both shook their heads. Solena chewed on her lip and sat down again, making me think she'd at least heard something. She might not know the entire story, but it was enough for her to know Meredith's words would have upset me.

"He saved my life. I'd met him and Knuckles earlier in the day at the bakery where I worked in the office. At the time, I couldn't hear as well as I do now, thanks to the new hearing aid the club bought for me. Knuckles had to sign as Truth spoke to me. We only met briefly."

"What does that have to do with you being here?" Casey asked. "I'm not being mean. I'm genuinely curious."

"Knuckles recognized me later that night. My brother had drugged me and taken me to Murphy's, where he tried to trade me to his dealer in order to lessen the debt he owed him. Knuckles called and told Truth." I held each of their gazes. "That man, the one you call an asshole, rushed to come save me. He threatened those men, brought me here, and kept me safe. He's done so much for me. I know I'm the new person here, but if anyone disrespects Truth in front of me again, I'm going to lose my shit."

I felt an arm come around my waist, and Truth's scent teased my nose. He tugged me against him, and I felt some of my anger and frustration drain away. How often did he hear stuff like that? Had they treated him like garbage all this time because he didn't automatically trust women? He hadn't told me about his past, but I had no doubt someone, if not multiple someones, had hurt him badly.

"Easy, Madison. I appreciate you sticking up for me, but it's okay. I've been pretty damn mean to most of the women I've come across. I warned you I wasn't a nice man."

I turned to look up at him. "But you are. Why can't everyone else see that?"

A man came over and I saw the word *President* on his cut. Had I gone too far? Was he going to be angry with me? If I got in trouble, would Truth have to pay the price for bringing me here?

"I see it," he said. "Truth has issues when it comes to women, but I also know he's changed since meeting you, Madison. You're right. He's a good man. Always has been, even if he's a bit rough around the edges."

"What's going on?" someone else asked.

"Your woman said Truth was an asshole to women and that she didn't think anyone would want him. It upset Madison," Casey said. "Can't really blame her. If someone said that about Maui, I'd have probably taken a swing at them."

"Well, so much for a fun family gathering," the man said. "It's nice to meet you, Madison. My name is Lynx, and I'm sorry for what Meredith said. She's mine and tends to have strong opinions. Once you get to know her better, you'll see that even when what she says sounds cruel, she doesn't mean it in a malicious way."

It felt like they were giving her a free pass, and I didn't understand. It didn't seem fair. I wanted them to see Truth the same way I did.

He kissed the top of my head and hugged me tight. "It's okay, Madison. I'm not bothered by what she said. The entire world can hate me, as long as you don't."

"Of course, I don't!" I reached up and placed my hand on his cheek. "I love you. I could never hate you."

His eyes darkened, and I realized I'd just confessed my feelings for him. I hadn't meant to. It just came out. My cheeks heated and I buried my face against his chest. Even worse. I'd done it in front of everyone. I wished the earth would open up and swallow me whole. How embarrassing!

"On that note, everyone grab a plate and get something to eat." I looked up in time to see Atilla reach for Solena and drag her off behind him. A few of the other men smirked at me, or even winked. I had a feeling they'd never let me forget this moment.

"Come on, honey. We'll get Liam and help him fix a plate too," Truth said, taking my hand. Then he leaned in close. "And for the record, I love you too."

What? I tripped over my feet with the shock of his words as he tugged me along in his wake.

Well, I certainly hadn't expected any of this to

happen when I'd woken up this morning. But Truth loved me... I couldn't remember a time I'd ever been happier.

* * *

Truth

The picnic hadn't gone as well as I'd hoped. I knew Meredith could be a bitch, but I thought Lynx had fixed her issues, or was helping her through them. She'd seemed to settle down and even started smiling more after they adopted the kids. Now I had to wonder if something else was going on that sent her spiraling again. Lynx had told us she didn't adjust well to changes. Was that all it was? Had me bringing Madison here tipped her over the edge? Or perhaps adding both Madison and Liam, and then not having a way to communicate with the little boy, had been too stressful and triggered an episode?

Both Madison and Liam were still asleep. The sun was barely up, and I had my first cup of coffee in my hand. My son's room wouldn't be completed for a little while, especially since Ravager had to handmake the train table we'd talked about. It did bother me that Liam didn't seem overly excited about being adopted. I'd stayed up last night watching videos after Madison went to sleep, trying to learn more sign language. Since it was the only way I could talk to my son, it was essential I learn as much as I could as quickly as possible. I wanted to show him I was trying to do what was necessary to take care of him.

My phone rang and I quickly answered, then realized no one in my family would have woken from the sound anyway. It was a bittersweet feeling. I couldn't believe I had a family of my own now, and yet, my wife could only partially hear with a hearing aid and my son couldn't hear at all. I wanted to give them the world, and it bothered me there was something I could never do for them -- give them both perfect hearing.

"Hello," I said, pressing the phone to my ear.

"It's Benson. Thought it would be best to call and not come by the compound."

"Yeah, might not be the best idea for you to show up at the gates. Although, it might be fun to watch the Prospect start to sweat as he figured out what to do. No way he'd call Atilla this early in the morning."

Benson laughed. "I have some good news for you. We passed over everything to the DEA. After answering some rather uncomfortable questions about the evidence we provided, they took Justin into custody. Got a call a few minutes ago saying he'd agreed to testify. They're going to have him under twenty-four-hour surveillance, and even have a private doctor who's going to help him get clean."

"That is awesome news. Thank you, Officer Benson."

"You can tell your woman her brother is going to be fine. Even I don't know where they're going to take him, but I know he's officially out of Bryson Corners. And there's one more thing."

"What's that?" I asked.

"While the DEA was doing some digging, they noticed the house was in his name. They did a bit of coaxing, and since Justin won't have the same identity when all this is over and can never return to the state of Oklahoma after the trial, he signed the house over to your wife."

I knew Madison would be overjoyed to own her family home. However, she couldn't live there. I didn't know what she'd want to do with the place. The neighborhood was decent. Maybe I could convince her to rent the property once we had it cleaned out and we'd done any repairs on the place. Something told me she wouldn't want to sell it.

"I appreciate that, and I know Madison will too."

"Her brother did write a note for her. I'll leave it, along with the papers for the house, with whatever man you have standing guard at the gate. You can give it to her when you think she's ready."

Before we hung up, maybe there was one more thing he could help me with. "Do you know anything about a little boy named Liam Nance? His father is Luca and his uncle is Angelo."

"Are you asking about his mother?" Benson asked softly. "That was seriously fucked up. We never could prove it was murder, but I'm almost certain it was. They claim a car jumped the curb and hit Liam's mother before crashing into a utility pole. Driver died on impact and his alcohol blood count was through the roof. Judge closed the case as a drunk driving accident."

"You think it was something more?"

"Yeah. I think Angelo Nance set it up, so he could lure his brother into helping him. It didn't take long after the mom died before Luca Nance went off the rails. On paper, he's a law-abiding citizen. We don't have anything that will stick in order to even bother arresting him. But I'm convinced he has his hands in his brother's business by now. Why do you ask?"

"Liam is our son now, but he didn't seem thrilled about the adoption. I was trying to figure out why."

Officer Benson grew quiet and when he finally spoke, I knew his thoughts were right about Liam's resistance to being here. "Take him to the cemetery. Visit his mother's grave, and make sure he understands you're trying to give him a safe and happy home, just the way his mother would have wanted."

"He knows she's dead, though, right? So why would he want to stay with Luca?" I asked. "It sounds like he's been a shitty father."

"I didn't give up on my dad until I was in my teens. It's possible if Liam had been with Luca that long, he'd have realized what sort of man he is. Right now, that little boy just wants his father's love, no matter what he suffers through to get it."

To some extent, I could understand. All boys looked up to their dads. Too bad for Liam he'd drawn the short straw. It didn't sound like his birth father gave a shit about him. But me? I did. I'd do whatever it took to prove it too.

"I'll take the family to visit Liam's mother. Madison can talk to him about her while we're there. What was her name?"

"Sonja Nance. Liam looks quite a bit like her. Thankfully, that boy won't look in the mirror one day and see Luca."

"Thanks, Officer Benson. I appreciate everything you've done. I can't speak for the club, but me personally, I owe you one."

He laughed. "Dangerous thing to say to a police officer."

We ended the call and I started on breakfast. By the time Madison and Liam woke up, I had omelets ready for all of us. They dug into their food, and I told Madison about the call I'd received. Although, I didn't tell her about the house or the note from her brother. Right now, we needed to focus on our son.

Cemeteries weren't places I opted to go. I'd always thought I'd avoid the place until I died. Looked like I was wrong. I stood behind Madison and Liam as they kneeled in front of Sonja's grave. Tears trickled down Liam's cheeks, and I wanted to wrap my arms around him and hold on tight. Instead, I stood back and gave the two of them some space. He trusted Madison already. With me, he remained a bit reserved.

She signed as she spoke, so I could hear what was being said.

"Your mother loved you very much, Liam. It made her sad when your dad didn't take care of you the way she'd wanted him to."

Liam signed something back. I thought he'd said he missed her.

"The only thing your mother wants is for you to be happy, safe, and loved. Your dad can't give you those things, Liam. When your mom died, it hurt him. You were both in pain, but he couldn't hug you the way you needed."

Liam said something else, and I didn't catch a word of what he'd signed. Whatever it was, it made Madison pause, and the look she shot my way was full of pain. She gave me a subtle tip of her head to come closer. I kneeled down behind the two of them.

"Truth isn't trying to replace your father, just like I'm not trying to replace your mother. They will always be your parents, but sometimes, bad things happen and we end up with more than one mother and father. Do you understand?"

Liam stayed quiet and still, but eventually gave a slight nod.

"Tell him that I'll be here to support him for as long as he needs me. I'm not asking for anything in return, except for him to follow the rules, do well in school, and live the kind of life that would have made his mother proud of him." She gave me a quick smile and signed what I'd said. Liam glanced at me over his shoulder. Slowly the boy turned and put his arms around my neck. I hugged him, and saw Madison was now crying as well.

"Everything is going to be fine," she said. "It may take him some time to adjust, but he's a good boy, Truth. Once he sees that he has a home with us, and that we won't push to replace the family he already had, then he'll come around."

* * *

Madison

It felt like everything wrapped up a little too neatly. Truth said my brother was going to get the help he needed, as well as a fresh start on life, and now I had the family I'd always wanted. Liam had even gone on a walk with Truth, leaving me behind. I hoped the two of them could bond. Truth might not be fluent in sign language, but he was learning, and I knew Liam appreciated it as much as I did.

I stood on the porch, waiting for them to return, and enjoying the sunlight. For the first time in years, I could breathe. I didn't have to look over my shoulder, sleep with one eye open, or worry about someone busting into the bathroom while I showered. All right, so Truth did tend to come in while I was showering, but it wasn't the same. I actually liked it when he joined me.

Movement to the right caught my attention. My joy dimmed a little when I saw Meredith coming toward me. She wasn't going to start something again, was she? Round two didn't sound like much fun.

"'Morning," she said, stopped at the foot of the steps. "Can we talk?"

"Mind if we stay out here? I'm waiting for Truth

and Liam to come back from their walk."

"They're at my house right now, playing with the kids. But sure, we can talk out here." She shoved her hands into her pockets. "About the picnic... I was out of line. It's common knowledge around here that I have a mental illness. Certain things can be a trigger for me. Not in a PTSD kind of way, but more like a mental meltdown. Sometimes that means I snap at people, say things I shouldn't, or go full out and act reckless. This has been a bad week for me. My dad died not too long ago. The pain has been unbearable, but usually I do okay. For whatever reason, I've felt his loss the most this week, and it sent me in a downward spiral. I was wrong to lash out at you about Truth, and I'm sorry. I already apologized to him too."

A mental illness? It amazed me she'd admit to having a problem. I also appreciated the fact she'd come to talk to me and apologized. At least she realized what she'd done was wrong.

"Thank you for coming to talk to me and putting your trust in me. I know it couldn't have been easy to say all that."

"Friends?" Meredith asked.

"I'd like that. You said Truth and Liam were at your house. We can walk there together, if you want?"

Meredith smiled and started walking. I remained at her side, and we talked a little more, until the sight in front of me stopped me in my tracks. Truth and Liam were sitting side by side while Meredith's kids were across from them. I watched as my husband helped Liam play with the children, using his limited sign language. It also broke my heart a little, knowing Liam would never be able to hear their voices or talk to them the way other children could. I'd been lucky, having at least partial hearing in one ear. Liam would never have that again. What would it be like to completely lose my hearing? I thought it would be rather terrifying, and lonely.

"Your son is rather remarkable," Meredith said. "Lynx and I spoke with Knuckles last night. He's going to offer sign language lessons to the children, and several of the adults are going to sit in too. Including me and Lynx."

"Thank you. It means a lot that everyone is willing to learn a new language in order to make Liam feel at home here."

"He's family. You both are."

Meredith put her arm around my shoulders, and I hugged her. I'd never had a friend before. In school, people were either downright rude, or overly polite. None had wanted to be a true friend to the deaf girl. It looked like Liam wasn't the only one getting a new life. I was too, all thanks to Truth.

I knew I'd never meet another man like him, no matter how long I lived. Truth was one of a kind, and I knew I was lucky to call him mine. All the women who'd treated him badly were idiots. As we'd lain in bed last night, he'd told me about the women who'd cheated on him, and we'd even talked about Jane. It wasn't any wonder he'd not trusted women for so long. He'd even said that he didn't think Jane would have stayed by him. I could tell her death weighed on him, but I'd do my best to help him move past it.

The road before us wouldn't always be smooth. We'd have bumps along the way, but together I knew we could get through anything.

Epilogue

Truth

I'd been gone all day, handling club business. Walking into a quiet house felt unsettling, especially since my wife and son were supposed to be here. I found Liam in his room, quietly playing with the train Ravager brought over a month ago. My boy had been here for five months, and we now had a good relationship.

He saw me in the doorway and smiled.

I'm back. Do you know where your mom is?

He quickly signed back, and his words made my stomach drop. *She's sick.*

I raced down the hall and into our bedroom. The sound of retching in the bathroom led me to Madison, where she hunched over the toilet. She'd been a little off the past week. No fever, but she'd felt queasy and certain smells made her run from the room. I'd begged her to see the doctor, but she'd been refusing.

"What's wrong?" I asked. "Is it the flu? Did you call the doctor?" I asked, reaching down to hold her hair back. I rubbed her back and waited while she caught her breath.

She pointed to the counter and I saw a stick on the surface. When I realized what it was, my heart nearly stopped. I picked it up and stared at the little display window. *Pregnant.* We were having a baby?

"Are you serious? You're pregnant?" I asked.

"I'll call the doctor tomorrow, but between my symptoms and that test, I'm going to say that yes, I'm definitely going to have a baby. I don't know how to tell Liam."

"We can figure that out later. Right now, what do you need from me?"

"Something to keep me from throwing up would be nice," she said.

"I think we have some crackers in the kitchen. I'll get them and a glass of water. Go lie down and I'll bring them to you."

She closed her eyes and let out a soft laugh. "Truth, I'm pregnant not dying. I'll come to the kitchen after I clean up."

On my way to get the crackers and water, I stopped to watch Liam for a moment. This house only had three bedrooms. I didn't want Madison to give up her library, and I couldn't ask Liam to share his room. Only thing I could think to do was add on to the house. And what if Madison wanted more children later?

It was a discussion we could have another time. In the kitchen, I grabbed the box of crackers, got her a glass of ice water, and sat to wait for her. When she came in and sat down, she had a little more color in her cheeks and looked better. She nibbled on the saltines and sipped the water.

"Are you happy?" she asked. "You'd wanted us to have a baby. Now we are."

Why did I feel like her question might be a trap? "Um. You and Liam were enough, but I can't lie. I'm excited about the baby. Worried about the changes we'll have to make, and how it will affect Liam. Concerned something could go wrong and we could lose the baby, or I could lose both of you. So… I guess I'm feeling a little bit of everything."

She reached over and took my hand. "Me too. But we'll get through it together. Nothing is impossible when we face it as a family, right?"

"Right." I leaned over the table to kiss her. "Love you, Madison. You, Liam, and now the baby are the best things that ever happened to me. I know I'm lucky to have you in my life, and I will do whatever it takes to give all of you the lives you deserve. All I want is for you to never regret coming here with me."

"That will never happen... Xander." I smiled at the use of my real name. It wasn't something she'd ever done until now. "I love you, and I'm right where I'm supposed to be."

She was right. No matter what happened, as long as we were together, everything would be fine. Madison was my one and only, and I'd give up my life for her if it came down to it. I finally had a family, and I was going to hold onto them with both hands and never let go.

Harley Wylde

Harley Wylde is an accomplished author known for her captivating MC Romances. With an unwavering commitment to sensual storytelling, Wylde immerses her readers in an exciting world of fierce men and irresistible women. Her works exude passion, danger, and gritty realism, while still managing to end on a satisfying note each time.

When not crafting her tales, Wylde spends her time brainstorming new plotlines, indulging in a hot cup of Starbucks, or delving into a good book. She has a particular affinity for supernatural horror literature and movies. Visit Wylde's website to learn more about her works and upcoming events, and don't forget to sign up for her newsletter to receive exclusive discounts and other exciting perks.

Bad Boys Multiverse
     A Bad Boy Romance
     Dixie Reapers MC
     Devil's Boneyard MC
     Hades Abyss MC
     Devil's Fury MC
     Reckless Kings MC
     Savage Raptors MC
     Devoted Guardians MC
     Owned by the Mob
     Bryson Corners
     Dixie Reapers MC Print Duets
     Dixie Reapers MC Audio

Harley at Changeling: changelingpress.com/harley-wylde-a-196

Changeling Press E-Books

More Sci-Fi, Fantasy, Paranormal, and BDSM adventures available in e-book format for immediate download at ChangelingPress.com -- Werewolves, Vampires, Dragons, Shapeshifters and more -- Erotic Tales from the edge of your imagination.

What are E-Books?

E-books, or electronic books, are books designed to be read in digital format -- on your desktop or laptop computer, notebook, tablet, Smart Phone, or any electronic e-book reader.

Where can I get Changeling Press E-Books?

Changeling Press e-books are available at ChangelingPress.com, Amazon, Apple Books, Barnes & Noble, and Kobo/Walmart.

ChangelingPress.com

www.ingramcontent.com/pod-product-compliance
Lightning Source LLC
Chambersburg PA
CBHW060552260626
47161CB00003B/1164